Birthday Book
2001-2002

Kylee Lin

REPTILE HOUSE

TYLE DRY CLEANERS

LAUGHATORIUM

HOUSE OF S-TYLE

SNAX SHAX

HALL OF TYLE

TRIAL
BY
~~JURY~~
Journal

OTHER BOOKS BY

Kate Klise

ILLUSTRATED BY

M. Sarah Klise

LETTERS FROM CAMP

REGARDING THE FOUNTAIN

TRIAL BY ~~JURY~~ Journal

Kate Klise

Illustrated by M. Sarah Klise

■ HARPERCOLLINSPUBLISHERS

Library of Congress Cataloging-in-Publication Data
Klise, Kate.
    Trial by journal / Kate Klise ; illustrated by M. Sarah Klise.
      p.   cm.
    Summary: In this illustrated novel told through journal entries, news clippings, and letters, twelve-year-old Lily finds herself on the jury of a murder trial while conducting her own undercover investigation of the case.
    ISBN 0-380-97880-6 — ISBN 0-06-029541-4 (lib. bdg.)
    [1. Trials—Fiction.   2. Jury—Fiction.   3. Murder—Fiction.
4. Diaries—Fiction.]   I. Klise, M. Sarah, ill.   II. Title.
PZ7.K684 Tr   2001   00-044866
[Fic]—dc21   CIP
                                                                                      AC

Typography by Sarah Klise
3 5 7 9 10 8 6 4 2

First Edition

TRIAL
BY
~~JURY~~
Journal

TYLEVILLE MIDDLE SCHOOL
Tyleville, Missouri

Mr. S. Holmes
Sixth Grade

November 3

Mr. and Mrs. Watson
221 Baker Street
Tyleville, Missouri

Dear Mr. and Mrs. Watson:

As of today, your daughter, Lily, has missed six full weeks of school during the first nine-week quarter.

I realize this was due to circumstances beyond her control. As the first juvenile juror in the state's history, Lily has not had an easy job. I'm sure schoolwork has been the last thing on her mind. And to be honest, I can't say I blame her, given the grisly nature of that terrible murder trial.

Unfortunately, making up six weeks' worth of schoolwork will be almost impossible. For this reason, I am recommending that you make plans now for Lily to attend summer school.

During the summer session Lily will be able to make up the work she missed this quarter, including the in-depth research paper that is a requirement of all sixth graders.

Please understand that I do not see summer school as a punishment. I, too, will be spending the summer months in school. (Such is the luck of first-year teachers.)

As you know, I had Lily in class for only three weeks before she left for jury duty. I look forward to getting to know her better when she returns for the second quarter. I especially hope she'll give the class a full report on what it was like to serve on a sequestered jury!

Sincerely,

S. Holmes

P.S. Lily's classmates will turn in their research papers on Monday, November 6. Please tell Lily that if she would like to try writing a research paper before she returns to school, I'd be happy to grade it. I don't want to discourage her or you, but it would be an enormous challenge for her to complete this project without the benefit of my instructions on how to outline, research, organize, and write a research paper. I mention this option only because I've been told by fellow teachers and by her classmates that Lily is a very *unique* student.

Monday, November 6, 5:35 a.m.

Dear Mr. Holmes,

I am so mad I could scream.

SUMMER SCHOOL???? Look, I didn't ask to be a juror in the Bob White trial. I didn't ask to get pulled out of school for six weeks. But now you're going to punish me by making me go to summer school? That. Is. So. Unfair.

And that's not even the worst part. After the Bob White trial ended, the lawyers wanted to read the journal you made me keep during jury duty. They said they had to see every stinking thing I wrote. Cripes! If I'd known anyone was going to read my journal, I never would've written **HALF** the stuff in here— especially the parts about me and my dumb teeth exercises.

At first it made me mad, but then it gave me an idea: If they could read the stuff I wrote during jury duty, why couldn't I read the stuff everybody ELSE wrote?

So I did. And here it is. I stayed up all night putting this research paper together. Luckily my mom saved the newspaper clippings about the trial for me. Leon said I could use his drawings, and Fawn let me borrow the first draft of her autobiography.

I got most of the other papers (the secret notes, dry cleaning tags, K-TYLE transcripts, etc.) from the prosecutors and FBI agents at Café Mongoose last night. They said they owed me a favor for helping them with the investigation.

2

Judge Gall gave me special permission to use all this stuff for my research paper, but he made me promise to return it "in perfect condition" to the courthouse as soon as you're done grading this. So PLEASE don't lose any of these papers or spill anything on them. (Sorry to sound so bossy, but this is evidence for the next trial.) Try to be really careful with Leon's drawings, too, because they could be valuable someday.

The pages from my journal are a total mess. I've never kept a journal before, so some of my early entries are really dumb. I don't know if this pile of papers even counts as a research paper. I'm only turning it in for one reason: I Do Not Want To Go To Summer School.

But even if I have to, please please P L E A S E don't make me stand in front of the class and give a corny old report about what it's like to serve on a jury or crack a criminal case. It would sound like I'm bragging and I'm not. I wasn't trying to save anyone's life (except maybe my own). And I sure didn't mean to turn Tyleville upside down. It just happened that way.

Well, never mind all that. The whole story is right here. And every single word is (unfortunately) the truth, the whole truth, and nothing but the truth.

Lily Watson

P.S. I have NO idea how to do footnotes or a bibliography, so you can forget about seeing any of that stuff in this research paper.

IN THE CIRCUIT COURT OF TYLE COUNTY, MISSOURI
Criminal Division

STATE OF MISSOURI)
)
Plaintiff,)
)
vs.)
)
R)   Case No. 123161
)
an)
)
AN)
)
)
Defendants.)

Thanks to
Judge E. Gall
for this!

ORDER GRANTING LEAVE TO WITHDRAW EVIDENCE

     The Court grants permission to Lily Watson to withdraw evidence for the purpose of completing a school research paper based on her experiences as the State's first Juvenile Juror.

     The evidence shall be returned to the Court immediately after Lily Watson's research paper has been read and graded so that the trial may proceed without delay.

     IT IS SO ORDERED.

Date: _November 5_

Judge E. Gall
Judge E. Gall
Tyle County Judge

LILY WATSON'S JOURNAL
AND

last minute

RESEARCH PAPER

(I'm too tired to think of a real title for this stupid thing)

PART ONE

Everything that happened
before the trial began,
including:

I.   The news of Perry's murder

II. Jury selection

III. Sequestration = living in a hotel ! ! !

I know I'm not doing this outline thing right, but you get the basic idea.

It all started in September when I got . . . THIS LETTER ☞

Circuit Clerk of Tyle County
Tyleville, Missouri

September 7

SUMMONS FOR JURY SERVICE

Ms. Lily A. Watson
221 Baker Street
Tyleville, Missouri

Dear Ms. Watson,

This letter is to notify you that your name has been selected for jury duty during this term of Court.

The Court has issued an order that you be present at the Tyle County Courthouse on Monday, September 25, at 8:00 A.M. for jury selection. You will be paid $5.00 each day you report to the courthouse.

Serving on a jury is one of the most important duties of citizenship. We hope the experience will be interesting and enlightening as you see your Court in action and participate in the process that is so fundamental to our democratic tradition of justice.

Sincerely,

C. Gull
Tyle County Circuit Clerk

MY JOURNAL

NAME: Lily A. Watson
GRADE: 6
TEACHER: Mr. Holmes
JOURNAL ENTRY FOR: Monday, September 25, 9:45 a.m.

Hi, Mr. Holmes!

How's everything at school? I wouldn't know since I'm not there. I'm sitting on a bench in a long hallway on the second floor of the Tyle County Courthouse, waiting for someone to tell me what the heck I'm supposed to do.

This is the first day of jury selection in the trial of Bob White. That means they're picking 12 people plus two alternates who will decide if Bob White killed Perry Keet.

Everyone knows Bob White did it. Everyone except maybe you, I mean. This all happened over the summer before you moved to Tyleville, so I'll fill you in on the details.

Perry was almost 12 years old, like me. (I just turned 12 last week. Yea!) He went to Tyleville Middle School and would've been in sixth grade this year, if he were still alive. Perry and I have been in the same class since kindergarten, but we weren't really friends. We weren't enemies either, but we sat at different lunch tables and did different things after school. Perry played soccer and was in the art club. I'm in band and work on the school newspaper.

Now that I think about it, Perry and I were engaged to be married for a couple of weeks in second grade. We had the starring roles that year in our class play, *Hansel and Gretel.* I think we called off the wedding during dress rehearsal. It was kind of a scandal (in a second grade way), but really it was just one of those dumb things you do when you're 8.

Anyway, Perry got a job last summer at Tyle Park Zoo, which is part of Tyle-O-Tropolis, the huge mall in downtown Tyleville. It's like an amusement park, circus and shopping mall, all in one. If you haven't already been, **GO**. It's the only fun thing we have in Tyleville.

I remember asking Perry how he got the job at the zoo. I always thought you had to be 16 years old to get a real job–besides baby-sitting or yard work, I mean. Perry told me he'd worked out a deal with Mr. Tyle, who owns Tyle-O-Tropolis. Perry said he volunteered to work for free doing anything (even gross stuff like cleaning out the cages) in exchange for free admission to the zoo whenever he wanted.

Mr. Tyle said OK. He even let Perry bring his friends to the zoo and sometimes gave them Tyle Tender to buy snacks. That's just how Mr. Tyle is. He's the richest guy in town, but he's not snobby or mean. He's really funny and generous. Mr. Tyle comes to school every year and tells stories about how he used to travel all over the world with a carnival. He performed magic shows for kings and queens in Europe. His specialty act was snake charming.

Mr. Tyle is nuts about snakes. He will give you $5 if you bring him a snake over four-feet long. Ask Joyce about the humongous **nine-foot black snake** she caught in third grade in the attic of the elementary school. She sold it to Mr. Tyle and he put it on display in the reptile house. Everyone went to the zoo to see it.

But don't waste your time going to Tyle Park Zoo to look for Joyce's snake. The reptile house has been closed for renovations since I was in fourth grade. Mr. Tyle is planning to build the biggest and fanciest reptile house in the world.

Besides, the biggest attraction at Tyle Park Zoo these days is Priscilla the gorilla. I'm SURE you've heard of her. She's the gorilla who's been painting all those modern pictures in her cage. It's the biggest story ever to hit Tyleville. People are coming from all over the country to see Priscilla and her famous paintings. We've even made the national news.

Unfortunately, Perry never got to see all that. Bob White killed Perry Keet before Priscilla started painting on the walls of her cage.

See, Bob White also worked at the zoo. His job was cleaning cages, too. But when Perry started working, he cleaned the cages faster and better than Bob. Then Bob got nervous about losing his job and killed Perry.

That's what everyone says, anyway. And that's why they're having this trial—to find out for sure what happened last summer. Twelve of the people at the courthouse today will be the jurors who decide if Bob White is guilty.

Speaking of the people here today, I have to tell you about the man sitting right here ◄——. He's eating tuna straight from the can. At 10 o'clock in the morning! **(P.U.)** I'm thinking of making a citizen's arrest.

We have a rule at my lunch table at school that no one can bring tuna for lunch. The smell is so strong, it makes everyone's lunch taste like cat food. I don't know if they have rules like that at the teachers' lunch table, but from my experience, you can't go wrong with peanut butter and jelly. Peanut butter and banana is a bit iffier. P.B. and honey is safe, too, but you probably already know all this from your last school.

There's another guy sitting here in the hallway who's been whistling nonstop all day. One cornball song after another. That's one thing that drives me crazy about grown-ups. If I sat here whistling, you can bet the bank someone would tell me to put a sock in it. But adults think they can share with the world any old tune that's dancing through their heads. I tried to make a face at him, like *"Sir, you're driving me crazy!"* But he just smiled and winked at me. **(Ugh.)**

News flash! Someone just came out of the circuit clerk's office and said we could all go home for the day, but we have to report back here tomorrow morning at 8 o'clock. I wonder if we still get $5 for coming today even though we didn't do anything.

I also wonder if I'm doing this journal thing right. I feel stupid, like I'm talking to myself. But you said just pretend like you're writing a letter, so that's what I'm doing.

I hope you like our class at Tyleville Middle School. And don't worry about snakes in the attic. There aren't any more up there. (I looked.)

More to follow from the Tyle County Courthouse.

Bye,

Lily

P.S. Nothing personal, but I think this journal assignment is a complete waste of time. I know I have to do something to make up for all the work I'm missing at school, but I HATE busywork. And that's what this journal thing is. Half the teachers at school assign work they never even read. When we get stupid assignments like that, I always write somewhere on my paper *blah blah blah* or *I bet you're not even reading this, are you?* or *Give me a sign if you're reading this.* They never are. Are you, Mr. Holmes?

yes

The Tyleville Quill

Tyle Publishing
Rhett Tyle, Publisher

50 cents..........................Monday, September 25.................Morning Edition

Jury selection begins today in trial of Bob White

Bob White

Perry Keet

Jury selection begins today in the trial of Bob White. White, 35, is charged with the abduction and murder of Perry Keet, 11, of Tyleville.

Keet, a volunteer at Tyle Park Zoo, disappeared from the zoo on July 24. His body was never recovered.

Prosecutors will argue that White murdered Keet and then disposed of the body. Although White initially confessed to police in July, he has entered a plea of not guilty. White remains in custody at the Tyle County Jail.

Priscilla the gorilla draws record crowds

Curiosity seekers from across the nation continue to flock to Tyle Park Zoo in Tyle-O-Tropolis to see Priscilla the gorilla. Yesterday proved to be a record breaker at the zoo. According to Tyle Park Zoo owner Rhett Tyle, more than 2,000 people purchased tickets to see Priscilla.

"We had people here from all over the map," Tyle said. "Everybody and his aunt Myrtle are coming to see this gorilla and have their picture taken with her."

Priscilla made headlines last month when red, yellow, and orange shapes were discovered painted on the walls of her cage. To encourage the gorilla's artistic expression, Tyle, an art lover, began providing Priscilla with paint, brushes, and dozens of blank canvases. Since then, Priscilla's paintings have evolved from the initial paint splatterings to more sophisticated works of abstract art, impressing art critics and animal lovers alike.

Priscilla's first painting in August

Tyle poses with Priscilla's latest paintings

What's the Buzz

by

Bernie "Buzz" Ard

Psst . . . This was supposed to be very hush-hush, but guess who came out of her gated estate over the weekend to see Priscilla the gorilla?

None other than Fawn Papillon, our most famous and reclusive neighbor. I'm told the former movie star, still ravishing at (whisper, whisper) 82, wore a scarf and dark glasses as she toured the zoo with her bodyguards.

Not being an animal lover myself–hey, I'd rather watch people!–I missed Ms. Papillon's appearance at the zoo. Haven't seen the doe-eyed starlet for months. Rumor has it she's working on her autobiography. Fawn's agent tells me the book will contain lots of juicy tidbits about Ms. Papillon's years in Hollywood before her return to Tyleville last year.

Nothing much else to report on the society front. I'm growing a bit weary of everybody going ape over this gorilla, but try saying that in public. They'd hang you in a heartbeat. Which reminds me of the Bob White trial. I've heard the men and ladies in blue have a signed confession from White, admitting he killed the boy. So who needs a trial?

Oh well, little thing called due process, I guess. Three guesses which way that drama's going to turn out. (And your first two guesses don't count.)

More gossip tomorrow. Till then,

That's the

"Buzz"

Parents, educators, and children's rights groups oppose juvenile juror law

Juvenile will serve on Bob White jury

The trial of Bob White will be of particular interest because of the presence of a juvenile on the jury. With the passage of the controversial juvenile juror bill last year, whenever a juvenile (someone under age 18) is the victim of a capital offense, one juvenile must serve on the jury.

In the White trial, lawyers will select one juvenile juror from a random pool of 15 Tyle County youths who received jury summonses earlier this month. The young person chosen to serve will have all the rights and responsibilities of an adult juror. Likewise, the juvenile juror will have to comply with the same restrictions as his or her adult counterparts. Because this jury will be sequestered, the juvenile juror will not be permitted contact with parents, teachers, or friends for the duration of the trial.

Parent organizations object to the forced parent-child separation. Education officials are unanimously opposed to the juvenile juror law because there are no provisions for tutoring or homework. "To pull a child out of school for weeks on end and say that a teacher cannot send homework is appalling," said Dr. Ed U. Caytor, superintendent of Tyleville Schools.

Others are against the juvenile juror law for psychological reasons.

"It's an outrage," said Lynn Goe, president of the Protect Our Children from What They Shouldn't Hear or See Organization, or POCFWTSHOSO for short.

"It's bad enough that one child has been murdered in this town," Goe said. "But to put another child on the jury and expose that child to the horror of the murder is a disgrace."

Goe and fellow members of POCFWTSHOSO plan to picket outside the courthouse.

MY AUTOBIOGRAPHY
BY
FAWN PAPILLON

Monday evening, late

I was boorrnnnnnnnnnnn–

Oh, poohf! How I hate this silly contraption! You hit one key too hardddddddd and the fool thing goes crazyyyyyyyyy.

I detest computers almost as much as I hateeeeeee (%#@) having to write this blasted autobiography. How I ever let my agent talk me into such a thing, I'll never know. But I've put it off long enoughhhhhhhhh (#!). Here we go. Curtain up.

CHAPTER ONE

I was born in a small town in Missouriiiiiiiiiiiiiiiiiiiiiiiiii.

Ach. Oh, good night!

MY JOURNAL

NAME: Lily A. Watson
GRADE: 6
TEACHER: Mr. Holmes
JOURNAL ENTRY FOR: Tuesday, September 26, 1:30 p.m.

I just reread my first journal entry. I sound like a lamebrain. I'd like to rip out the whole thing and start over, but I remember you said the three rules for keeping a journal are:

1) Write what you think.
2) No erasing.
3) No do overs.

How are you grading this journal, anyway? Not that I'll try any less if it's pass/fail, but I like to know these things up front. Knowledge is power. That was the theme of our fifth grade homecoming skit. Don't even ask what place we got in the competition. (OK, we got dead last. Our class is so pathetic sometimes, it's just plain embarrassing.)

So anyway, I'm sitting on the same bench in the hallway of the Tyle County Courthouse. Some big shots (you can tell by their clompy shoes) are walking up and down the hall, going in one room and coming out another.

The tuna guy is back. He's been playing solitaire all morning. The whistler is sitting next to him. Only he's not whistling now. He's FLOSSING his teeth—right in front of everyone. That guy wouldn't last five minutes in sixth grade. Neither would a lady here who's wearing sunglasses (inside) and the biggest, craziest hat you've ever seen in your life. It's got a fake bird sitting on top of it! Please, lady. Save the costume for Halloween.

Another man is drawing in a sketch pad. I recognize him. He's got a shop downtown called Paintings by Leon. He's really good. I looked at his sketch pad when I walked to the vending machines. (I was starving, so I bought some pretzels and a root beer.)

By the way, I should warn you: Don't *ever* buy orange soda at school. I don't know why, but everyone makes complete fun of people who drink orange soda. I made the mistake of buying it once in fourth grade. BIG mistake. Don't do it!

(I hope you don't mind me making these suggestions, but I figure since you're a new teacher, you might not know these things.) Much appreciated

Back to the business at hand. In my last entry, I told you a little about Perry Keet. Now I'll tell you about the guy who killed him: Bob White.

The first thing about Bob is that he's not too smart. I don't think he even made it through middle school. Before all this happened, I'd see him riding his beat-up old bike along the highway into town. Even in the rain, he rode that thing. And he always wore ratty clothes with patches all over them. He looked like a creepy old clown.

Another thing about Bob White is that he has that *old man smell.* I don't know why. He's the same age as my uncle Jim—35 years old. The reason Bob smells so bad is because he's always dirty. My mom says he probably doesn't have running water out in the trailer where he lives, so I bet he never takes showers or baths. Plus, his job was cleaning cages at the zoo, which doesn't help much in the smell department.

Bob White was on my route last year when I had to sell magazine

subscriptions for band. That's all you do in band—sell stuff
nobody wants, like magazines and cheap candy and lightbulbs.
Two years ago we had to dress up as chickens and sell frozen
chicken breasts door-to-door. Completely humiliating.

Anyway, last year I rode my bike out to Bob's trailer north of town
to see if he wanted to buy any magazine subscriptions. I thought
he might like a subscription to *Dog Breeder* or *Bark* since he
has so many dogs. I'd guess about 38.

But, cripes, you should see his place! It's covered with old brown
paneling, like my friend Sally has in her basement. But Bob
White has it on the outside of his trailer, where it doesn't really
hold up too well against the weather. His roof is just an old piece
of rusty tin. There are tall weeds growing everywhere and empty
dog food cans scattered all over the place.

In a way, I'm glad I went there because I'd never seen a house
like that before. Of course I didn't sell any magazine subscriptions
to Bob. Turns out he can't even read. He told me so himself.
He said he could read road signs like STOP and YIELD. And he
can tell the difference between BEEF and CHICKEN on dog
food cans. But that's about it. I asked him if he could write
and he said, "Well, I writes some but I doubts anyone else can
read it."

I still can't believe that. My mom and dad would **KILL** me if
I got that old and couldn't read or write. I mean, it's sad, but
that's no excuse for Bob White to kill Perry Keet. Maybe I
shouldn't jump to conclusions (especially since I might be a juror),
but it's hard not to when everyone knows he did it.

It's a bad deal all around. I do feel a little sorry for Bob White.
But I feel more sorry for Perry. I can't even imagine what it must

be like to die, especially when the person killing you has B.O. as bad as Bob White.

I also feel sorry for Mr. Tyle. He must feel awful about the whole thing. If he hadn't hired Bob White to work at the zoo, none of this would have happened. I hope this doesn't mean Mr. Tyle will stop visiting our school. I love his magic tricks, especially the one where he makes a live bird hatch out of an omelet. And he tells the world's best stories.

Once Mr. Tyle told us about the time he got invited to dinner at Buckingham Palace in London. He found out from the royal chef that they were having roast duck for dinner. So, on his way to the palace, Mr. Tyle bought a live duck and **hypnotized it with his eyes.** He plucked all the feathers off it and hid the duck under his coat. When he arrived at the palace, he snuck into the royal kitchen and switched the cooked duck with the hypnotized duck. Then Mr. Tyle smothered the hypnotized duck with warm gravy so it looked like the real dinner.

Can you guess what happened when they all sat down to dinner? Mr. Tyle snapped his fingers and the hypnotized duck woke up and flew off the plate! I'm laughing out loud just picturing the Queen of England when she saw her dinner flying around the royal dining room.

Mr. Tyle says he can hypnotize anyone or anything. Next time he comes to school, I'm going to ask him to hypnotize someone from our class. Or maybe a teacher. Maybe an English teacher who assigns busywork journal projects. No offense, but you know what I mean, jelly bean. (I love sneaking in dumb stuff like that on assignments I know teachers never read.)

Wait . . . you're not going to believe this. That same guy as yesterday came out of the circuit clerk's office and said we could all go home for the day, but we have to report back here AGAIN tomorrow morning at 8 o'clock.

I think I'll walk over to Tyle-O-Tropolis and see Priscilla the gorilla. More later.

Have a pretzel, Mr. Holmes.

Thank you.

SEPTEMUR 27

I DINDT DO IT. REELY I DINDT. I DONT NO HOW
TO MAKE IT ENNY MORE CLEARRER THEN THET.

BUT I DINDT KILL THAT BOY. PEEPUL THINKS JEST CAWZ
YOUR DUM THEN YOU MUST BE BAD TO. BUT IM
NOT THAT WAY. I MIGHT LIKE GOOD SENS BUT I
AINT BAD. SPESHLY WHEN IT COMES TO PERRY. HE
WAZ A NIZE BOY. I YUSED TO SEE HIM LAST SUMUR
CLEENING OUT THE GORILLYS CADGES. HE WAS ALWEYS
HAPPY AND SMILLING. I WOODNT NEVER KILL
NOBODY LIKE THAT. I WOODNT NEVER KILL NOBODY.
BUT WHOS GOIN TO BELIVE ME? NOBODY THETS WHO.

MY JOURNAL

NAME: Lily A. Watson
GRADE: 6
TEACHER: Mr. Holmes

JOURNAL ENTRY FOR: Wednesday, September 27, 10:45 a.m.

I counted all the people who showed up at the courthouse this morning. Including me, there are 207 people here. We all got the same letter, telling us to come to the courthouse. Now we're waiting to find out who will be on the jury.

They'll pick 12 jurors, plus two alternates in case someone gets sick or is kicked off the jury. One of the jurors has to be under 18 because of that new law. I don't know if I have a chance at this thing or not. I think the other kids gave better answers to the lawyers' questions.

Before we met the lawyers, we had to fill out questionnaires about who we are and what we do. I don't know why. Probably the lawyers are just being nosy. It's like new teachers who pass out surveys and make us write where we live and what our parents do. Really they just want to know whose parents are rich and which kids they should be nice to. It's so obvious.

My dad is a barber and my mom works at Tyle Mercantyle, which is fine with me. But on those nosy teacher questionnaires I like to write that my dad is a crowned prince of Bohemia and my mom is ambassador to Andorra and that we have castles too numerous to count. I also write that I have six brothers and six sisters who are in boarding school in Namibia. (Really, I'm an only child.)

Anyway, on the jury questionnaire, where it asked for my

occupation I wrote "student." I thought about putting "baby-sitter," but I do that only on weekends. After we finished answering the questions, we went into a big room and watched a video about jury duty. Complete snorification. The tuna guy even fell asleep. During the video, I could see the lawyers looking at our questionnaires. When it was over, they told us to go back into the courtroom so they could ask us more questions. That's when it got interesting.

Interesting and creepy, I should say, because guess who was there? BOB WHITE. He was sitting on a wooden chair, right in the middle of the courtroom, with guards on either side of him.

He looked just like I remember, only a little cleaner. They must've made him take a shower in jail. He was wearing an orange jumpsuit, but he still had that mangy-dog look. I'd forgotten what his eyes look like—kind of clear and watery. And his teeth are brownish yellow and *crazily crooked*. His teeth are ten times worse than mine, which are so-so crooked, but I've been doing exercises to straighten them.

The lawyer who will try to prove Bob White killed Perry is named Golden Ray Treevor. He looks like a guy you'd see on TV. He was wearing a fancy dark-blue suit and yellow suspenders. He spoke V E R Y . . . S L O W L Y . . . A N D . . . S E R I O U S L Y like a TV newscaster. He's what they call a prosecutor. He also had a weird smell.

Mr. Treevor told us this was a first-degree murder case. That means if the jury decides Bob White is guilty, he could get the death penalty during the sentencing phase of the trial. Mr. Treevor asked in a real low, serious voice: "C O U L D . . . Y O U . . . C O N D E M N . . . A . . . M A N . . . T O . . . D E A T H ?"

He asked this to each person in the room. Because of the way he talks, it took about a half hour. When he finally came to me, I said I could, but that it would probably give me the creeps. Mr. Treevor said it was OK if it gave me the creeps as long as I could do it. He asked me again, and I said, "Yes."

I felt a little weird saying that in front of Bob White. But it's the truth. If he killed Perry Keet, he has to die. It's only fair. Think how awful it must be for Perry's mom and dad to know the man who killed their son is still alive. Even if you put him in jail, he could still escape. (And I bet you he'd try.) It's just too dangerous to have someone that creepy and stinky on the loose.

(I just remembered what Mr. Treevor smells like. Cigars. **BLEH**.)

The lawyer defending Bob White is named Mally Mute. NOT Molly, she told us. It's Mally—short for Mallory. She's a public defender, which means she gets paid to work FOR Bob White, but not BY him, since he's "financially challenged," as Ms. Mute put it. I heard someone behind me ask what that meant. The tuna guy said real loud, **"He's dirt poor and everyone knows it."**

The whole time I was trying not to look at Bob White, but when the tuna guy said that, my eyes swung over in Bob's direction without me even thinking about it. And there was Bob, just looking down at his hands, like he was more embarrassed by being poor than he was for being a murderer, which is REALLY vomitous. He didn't look one bit sorry for what he did to Perry.

Mally Mute looks young—maybe the age of my aunt Julia (28)—and serious, too. Turns out, Ms. Mute could've gotten this trial moved to another county, but she didn't. She said she thinks the people in Tyle County are some of the smartest and fairest

24

in the whole state. She said if Bob White couldn't get a fair trial here, he wouldn't get one anywhere.

I think she was trying to butter us up with that kind of talk, but I guess that's her job. The truth is, everybody in the whole STATE heard about Perry's murder, so Tyle County's probably as good a place as anywhere to have the trial.

Ms. Mute asked if there was anyone in the room who wouldn't accept that a person was innocent until proven guilty. She said our whole system of criminal justice is based on that simple idea. She also said it was OK if someone in the courtroom didn't believe that. She just needed those people to raise their hands and tell her so.

Not a single hand went up, which I couldn't believe. Everyone KNOWS Bob White is guilty. Maybe I should've raised my hand, but I didn't want to be the only one. Besides, I thought about it for a minute and figured maybe she's right. Even if he is guilty, he should at least get a trial. That's how they do it on TV, anyway.

When no one raised a hand, Ms. Mute started talking again. She said it's up to Mr. Treevor to prove Bob White is guilty beyond a reasonable doubt. What that means is that Bob White doesn't have to prove one dang thing. She asked if there was anyone who didn't believe that's how it should work. No hands.

Then she asked us if we could ignore what we've heard about the case and base our decision on the evidence from the trial. She also told us about the deliberation process, which is at the end of the trial when the jury has to decide if Bob is guilty. Her question to us was: "If 11 jurors think Bob White is guilty, but the evidence left some reasonable doubt in your mind, would you have the courage to stand by your beliefs and vote not guilty?"

She asked us this one by one, just like Mr. Treevor did earlier. Whenever she came to a kid, she said it might be especially hard for us to stand up for what we believed. When she came to me, I told her I thought I could do it because I don't let anybody push me around too much. She smiled and said she could tell. That was nice of her. I wonder if she's married. My aunt Julia isn't married. Are you? (Am I even allowed to ask questions in this journal? I still don't think I'm doing this right.)

No. Yes. You're doing fine.

Whoops. I've got to run. The lawyers just called us back into the courtroom. More nosy questions, I bet. I'll write more later.

Lily

P.S. I almost forgot to tell you: Turns out this is going to be a sequestered jury. I had to ask the lady sitting next to me—who keeps trying to READ OVER MY SHOULDER, MIND YOUR OWN BEESWAX, LADY!—how to spell "sequestered." What that means is that the jury gets to stay in a hotel in Tyleville and eat all their meals at restaurants for as long as this trial lasts. If I get on the jury, I'm going to order shrimp cocktail every night. I had that once in Florida, and I swear I could live on those things!

FROM THE DESK OF MALLORY MUTE
Public Defender
Tyle County, Missouri

JURY FOR BOB WHITE TRIAL

JUROR NAME	AGE	OCCUPATION
1. Bernie "Buzz" Ard	64	newspaper columnist
2. Fawn Papillon	82	actress (retired)
3. Leon D. Vinci	31	artist
4. Sy Meese	58	truck driver
5. Leland Earl (L. E.) Font	50	orthodontist
6. Kim Illion	33	hairstylist
7. Sandy Piper	44	teacher
8. Mia Sparrow	21	stay-at-home mother
9. Don Key	75	florist (retired)
10. Woody Pecker	52	furniture store owner
11. Anna Conda	48	fashion designer
12. Lily Watson (juvenile juror)	12	student

ALTERNATES

1. Willy Mammoth	89	furrier (retired)
2. Penny Gwen	37	sales rep, tuxedos

Name: *Anna Conda*
Address: 7 Diamondback D... OKA...
Age: 48
Occu...
Tyle...
Have y...
Do you...
Abss...

Name: Fawn Papillon   U.ES!
Address: Papillon Estate
A...
O...
H...
c...
D...
y...

Name: Lily A. Watson   YES
Address: 221 Baker Street
Age: 12
Occupation: student
Have you followed media coverage of the Bob White case? Kind of.
Do you believe you could be a fair and impartial juror in this trial?
I think so.

The Tyleville Quill

Tyle Publishing
Rhett Tyle, Publisher

50 cents.........................Saturday, September 30.................Morning Edition

Jury selected in Bob White trial; Columnist Bernie "Buzz" Ard to serve

After five days of questioning by attorneys, a jury was selected late yesterday to hear the murder trial of Bob White. Six men, five women, and one 12-year-old girl will serve as jurors in the trial, which will begin next week.

In a press conference held yesterday, *Tyleville Quill* society columnist Bernie "Buzz" Ard announced that he was among the selected jurors. Buzz also said he would continue to write his column during the trial.

"Hey, it's the least I can do for my loyal fans," Buzz said. "Besides, there's bound to be good material. Just think: Twelve jurors and two alternates forced to live and work together to determine the fate of a man charged with killing a young child. It doesn't get much heavier than this, folks."

Buzz was granted special permission to continue writing his column by Judge E. Gall, who called *The Quill* columnist "Tyleville's favorite man-about-town."

To maintain the tight security required during sequestration, the court will provide an armed guard to deliver Buzz's column from the hotel where jurors will live during the trial to *The Quill* offices.

During the press conference, Buzz predicted the story of the jurors might prove more interesting than the trial itself.

"The prosecution's case is tighter than a drum," Buzz said. "Besides, it's the story behind the story that always interests me." (See "What's the Buzz" on page 2.)

Priscilla's animal magnetism attracts crowds

Priscilla wows crowds

Her story has been told in newspapers across the nation. Her image has appeared on cereal boxes and billboards.

But don't expect Priscilla the gorilla to cop a star attitude. The celebrated artist still works for bananas in her newspaper-lined cage at Tyle Park Zoo. And her favorite activity, other than painting, seems to be posing for pictures.

Critics argue that all this attention could interfere with Priscilla's artwork.

"Nonsense," says zoo owner Rhett Tyle.

"Priscilla paints at night, after the zoo closes," Tyle explained. "She doesn't like painting in front of people. Call it artistic temperament. That's just the way she is."

Temperamental or not, Priscilla's personality continues to endear her to legions of fans, many of whom travel hundreds of miles to see this amazing gorilla and her remarkable paintings.

What's the Buzz
by
Bernie "Buzz" Ard

Believe-it-or-noddity: Guess where I'm heading? That's right. The Bob White trial. Jury duty. To perform my civic duty. Life. Death. Guilt. Innocence.

Heavy stuff, huh? So what to pack for this assignment? I'm thinking cruisewear.

And here's the big news: I can't reveal the names of my fellow jurors (and it's killing me!), but I'll tell you this much: We've got a star-studded lineup here to beat the band.

Think local celebrity recluse. Starving artist. Fashion designer. And those are just three of the jurors! Wowie kazowie. This is what the suits in Hollywood call an "ensemble cast."

I'll keep you posted with regular behind-the-scenes updates from the trial. I'll tell you who's hot, who's not. Where the "in" jurors are vacationing this winter. You know the drill. And I'll be there till the bitter end.

Speaking of endings, I'll bet no one in town will be happier to see the tail end of this saga than Rhett Tyle. It was Tyle, remember, who gave Bob White the job at the zoo.

And speaking of movers and shakers, Rhett Tyle and Anna Conda (he's the mover, she's the shaker) have been quite the cozy couple lately. Wasn't that Anna's lipstick I saw on your collar Friday night, Rhett? In the corner booth at Rhettalini's?

That's my verdict anyway.

Next report from behind the curtain of sequestration at the trial of the century.

(Continued on page 30, column 1)

Protestors prepare for trial

Like Priscilla the gorilla, members of Protect Our Children from What They Shouldn't Hear or See Organization (POCFWTSHOSO) will spend the weekend painting. But their mission is anything but monkey business.

"We take this very seriously," said Lynn Goe, president of POCFWTSHOSO, the organization formed to protest the juvenile juror law.

Goe and her fellow POCFWTSHOSO members are creating signs and banners to carry outside the courthouse during the Bob White trial.

"A child is neither mentally nor emotionally strong enough to sit on a jury that decides a murder case," explained Goe. "It's cruel and unusual punishment to subject a child to this. Our members are prepared to picket outside the courthouse all day every day for as long as the Bob White trial lasts."

Protestors plan to picket

(From page 2)

Hoo boy! We haven't had an honest-to-goodness trial in this town for years. Buckle your seat belt and hold on tight.

We'll be burning the scandal at both ends.

Now this is my kind of story!

"Buzz"

MY AUTOBIOGRAPHY
BY
FAWN PAPILLON

CHAPTER ONE

Saturday, late

As I gaze out my French doors overlooking Tyleville, I remember my early days in this town when . . . when . . . when I was not such an OLD FOOL!

Have mercy! What an atrocious opening paragraph. I had no idea this writing business was so difficult. Especially beginnings. Where to start? Childhood? My first film at the tender age of 12? My dramatic (ho, ho) retirement 50 years ago?

Oh, crumb. This is frightful torture. Like trudging onstage for Act I in high heels with blisters on both feet.

Maybe being sequestered in a hotel for a few weeks will help me focus my thoughts and memories. Memories? Bah. I can't remember what I had for breakfast this morning. What cruel beast invented old age? Better take along a box of old photos to jog this sluggish memory.

Of course, I won't be able to work on this cockamamie autobiography during the day when I'm on jury duty. But at night I must write for at least one hour. Yes, every night for one hour. Discipline! Resolve! Willpower! (Where's my chocolate stash?)

I shall toil away, writing something worth reading. Surely it can't be worse than being written about by the Hollywood hacks and gossip columnists. If those stooges can write, I can too. By golly, I can! I'll show themnsz4zzzzz.

Well, pllzfstz. Never mind this qazxcompoo ter. I'll finish this autobiography if it's the last thing I do.

Now where's my suitcase? I must remember to pack my bath oils and Madame's doggie shampoo and biscuits. I do hope the hotel allows pets.

MASTER OF THE MARVEL   AMBASSADOR OF THE ENIGMA

RHETT TYLE

❮❮﹠❯❯

"The Man with the Million-Dollar Smile!"   Chief Executive Officer, Tyle Enterprises

From the Penthouse Suite of the Majestic Tyle-O-Tropolis

Tyle Park Zoo	Tyle Entertainment	Tyleville Bank	Tyle Communications
Tyle Snax Shax	Tyle Pie-Thon Bakery	Tyle Properties	Tyle Dry Cleaners
Tyle Trinkets	Tyle Exterminators	Tyle Publishing	Tyle Mercantyle

October 3

The Honorable Judge E. Gall
Tyle County Courthouse
Tyleville, Missouri

Dear Judge,

Today is your lucky day! I know you've been up to your eye-balls in the Bob White trial. As Tyleville's First Citizen, I want you to know I think you're doing a Tyle-riffic job! Three cheers for Judge E. Gall!

But with all this legal-beagle stuff on your plate, I'll bet you haven't had time to think about where you're going to put the jurors during the trial. Let me help.

As you know, I own The Menagerie Hotel, the world's finest animal-themed hotel in the magnificent Tyle-O-Tropolis complex. I can make an entire floor of the hotel available to the jurors for as long as the trial lasts. The rooms are spacious and comfortable. The security is tight. And, best of all, I'm willing to donate these accommodations as part of my ongoing mission to bring justice and closure in the tragic death of Perry Keet.

See what I mean about this being your LUCKY DAY? I'll even throw in meals at any of the six world-class restaurants conveniently located in Tyle-O-Tropolis AND free tickets to Tyle Park Zoo, just a short elephant ride away from The Menagerie Hotel.

The jurors in the Bob White trial deserve the very best. It would be my great honor to have these fine Tyleville citizens stay at The Menagerie Hotel, where I always promise my guests an unforgettable experience.

Hope you'll consider my offer. It's the least I can do for the people of this great city, who work at the 438 businesses owned and operated by Tyle Enterprises, the largest, most generous, and now the only employer in Tyleville.

Justice for all! *Rhett Tyle*

HIGH WIRE ACT*

AND SIX WORLD-CLASS RESTAURANTS

PLUS COUNTLESS SHOPS & BOUTIQUES

*EVERY HOUR!

MARCHING BANDS*

AND THE MENAGERIE HOTEL

ALL THIS AND MORE WAITING FOR YOU AT TYLE-O-TROPOLIS!

TYLE PRINTING AND PUBLISHING

KEN AIRY: From the majestic studios of K-TYLE atop Tyle-O-Tropolis in downtown Tyleville, this is Ken Airy with K-TYLE news on the hour. K-TYLE TV reporter Maggie Pie is standing by with breaking news. Maggie?

MAGGIE PIE: Ken, I'm here on the steps of the Tyle County Courthouse, where just minutes ago the twelve jurors and two alternate jurors chosen for the Bob White trial were whisked away in two unmarked vans. I'm told by reliable sources that the jurors are en route to a local hotel, where they'll be sequestered for the duration of the trial.

KEN AIRY: Do we have any idea where the jurors will be staying, Maggie?

MAGGIE PIE: No, Ken. All we know is that they have reservations somewhere nearby.

KEN AIRY: Remind us again why this jury is being sequestered.

MAGGIE PIE: The prosecution is seeking the death penalty for Bob White for the murder of Perry Keet. State law requires that jurors in death penalty cases be sequestered -- that is, secluded -- during the trial. It's a way to shield jurors from media coverage of the trial, which could influence their decision.

KEN AIRY: I see.

MAGGIE PIE: A sequestered jury is also less

likely to be swayed by public opinion, which is very strong in this case.

KEN AIRY: What are you hearing from locals, Maggie?

MAGGIE PIE: Let's ask some innocent passersby. Excuse me, ma'am. Can you tell me your feelings about Bob White and his possible involvement in the death of Perry Keet?

UNIDENTIFIED WOMAN: There's no question in my mind. He did it.

MAGGIE PIE: What makes you so sure?

UNIDENTIFIED WOMAN: How else do you explain a little boy disappearing from the zoo? They never even found his body. But I saw that Bob White on TV. He was cagey and his eyes were small and beady, just like a killer's. The eyes always give 'em away.

MAGGIE PIE: Thank you. And, sir, how about you? What do you think Bob White's chances are of being found not guilty?

UNIDENTIFIED MAN: Oh, I'd say about 17 billion to one. Everybody knows he did it. He told the police himself he did it. Now he's trying to backpedal his way out of it. If you ask me, I think that's disgusting.

MAGGIE PIE: There you have it, Ken. Back to you.

KEN AIRY: Thank you, Maggie. And just a reminder to our listeners that Maggie Pie and her Tyle-Cam reports can be seen on K-TYLE TV, a satellite service available only through Tyle Entertainment, a property of Tyle Enterprises.

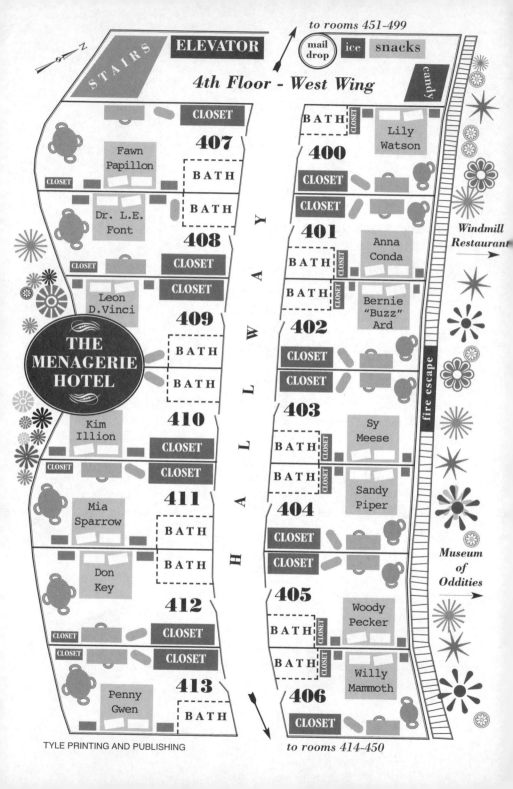

THE MENAGERIE HOTEL
Tyleville, Missouri
A Tyle Entertainment Property

Dear Guest,

Welcome to The Menagerie Hotel. My name is Robin and I will be your housekeeper during your stay.

I hope your visit is a relaxed and comfortable one. If you have any special requests, please leave me a note. Stationery can be found in the top drawer of your desk.

Tyle Dry Cleaners has offered to provide free, one-hour dry cleaning and laundry service for jurors in the Bob White trial. You may leave your laundry in the mini-closet built into the door to your room.

I look forward to providing you with the hospitality that has long been associated with this fine hotel. I have every confidence that your stay at The Menagerie Hotel will be an unforgettable experience.

Sincerely,

Robin

Housekeeping Department

P.S. The Tyle Tender on your desk is courtesy of the management. This money can be used at any of the shops or fine restaurants in Tyle-O-Tropolis. Please see the dining guide on your desk for more information.

39

NAME: Lily A. Watson
GRADE: 6
TEACHER: Mr. Holmes
JOURNAL ENTRY FOR: Thursday, October 5, 4:45 p.m.

This is the coolest hotel in the whole world.

I was here once a million years ago for my aunt Elizabeth's wedding. Don't even ask about my performance as a flower girl. (One word: disaster.) The wedding was held in the Japanese garden outside, but I never went inside the hotel. It is beyond belief!

The main lobby has shiny marble floors and big, golden cages filled with exotic birds, like macaws and cockatoos. In the middle, there's a fountain with fish and ducks. (Live ducks!) Everywhere you look in the hotel, there are flowers and trees and birds and waterfalls. It's like a beautiful fairy-tale jungle.

The jury is staying on the fourth floor. To get there, you take an old-timey elevator that looks like a metal cage. On the way up, you pass the second floor. That's where the swimming pools are. We stopped to take a peek and I nearly fainted. I counted 16 pools, but there might be more than that. All the pools are different sizes and shapes, and they're all surrounded by beautiful birds in fancy cages. The water in each pool is a different color (pink, blue, green, yellow) and temperature (chilly, chilly-warm, warm, warm-hot, etc.). I hope we get to go swimming every night!

(**RATS!** I forgot to pack my swimsuit. Maybe I can buy one in the gift shop.)

When you get off the elevator at the fourth floor, my room is the first door on the left. All the doors curve outward because each door has a secret little closet WITHIN the door where you can leave your dirty laundry for the cleaners. Cool, huh?

In my room, there's a double bed with a night table on each side. I've got a sofa, two closets, and my own bathroom. I've also got my own personal air conditioner. (My parents won't let me touch the controls on the one we've got at home.) I've also got a desk and chair, in case I want to do any school stuff while I'm here. Ha ha ha ha ha ha ha.

But here's the best part. Every room on this floor has a different animal theme. I'm staying in the zebra room, so my bed looks like a sleeping zebra. My curtains have black-and-white zebra stripes. Same with the shower curtain and towels. And there's a black-and-white striped bathrobe and a pair of slippers for me to wear, plus little bars of zebra-striped soap AND zebra-y bottles of shampoo and conditioner.

This is exactly the kind of hotel my family never stays at because my mom would call it "too too." I always ask, "Too too what?" And she says, "Just too too." Cripes, what kind of reason is that?

I almost forgot the most wonderful thing. There's a lady here named Robin who will clean my room for me every day. I am IN HEAVEN!

At 6 o'clock tonight I'm meeting the rest of the jurors for dinner. We're eating downstairs in Le Tyle. That's the fanciest restaurant in town. I hope they have shrimp cocktail.

I already know some of the jurors. Leon D. Vinci is here. He's the artist I saw drawing in the hallway of the courthouse. And guess who else is here? The tuna man! His name is Sy Meese and he's in the room three doors down from me. He has a big droopy mustache (gross) with little bits of food always hanging in it (grosser) AND ear hair (grossest!).

And here's the big news: Staying right across the hall from me is—*ta dah!*—Fawn Papillon. I *know* you know her name. She's the famous movie star who grew up here and then went off to Hollywood. It was a really big deal when she moved back to Tyleville last year. But she almost never comes out of her house, so no one knows much about her.

Turns out it was Ms. Papillon who was wearing that crazy bird hat in the hallway of the courthouse. When I was checking in, I saw her wearing the same hat in the lobby. She had on dark sunglasses and she was carrying a little dog. I don't know what kind it is, but it's really tiny and cute and has floppy ears. Ms. Papillon let me pet it and told me her name is Madame.

Then, when I got upstairs I saw Ms. Papillon moving her suitcases into the room across the hall from mine. She said, "Well, here we are, fa la la!" in a funny, singsongy voice that made me laugh. She's completely weird, but I like her.

I'll write more later. Here's a postcard of The Menagerie Hotel. (If you don't mind, I'd like it back for my scrapbook.)

The Menagerie Hotel

Creature Comforts

Princely Pleasures

Animals Always Welcome

6,000 Rooms
All with a View of
The Magnificent
Tyle-O-Tropolis

World's **Only** Swan-Shaped Swimming Pool  **SIX** World-Class Restaurants Shopping, Entertainment & So Much **More!**

MY AUTOBIOGRAPHY
BY
FAWN PAPILLON

CHAPTER ONE

Thursday night

Unpacked. Bathed. Hair washed. Madame brushed. Clothes set out for first day of jury duty.

Now, to the book. Possible titles:

~~My Life~~
~~My Pitiful Little Life~~
~~The Story of An Old Bat Like Me~~
~~Reflections (On My Life)~~

Oh, for pity's sake. This IS dreadful. Absolutely dreadful. Though I am starting to get the hang of this computer-rrrrrrr. (Strike that.)

Now if I could just think of something to write. Something interesting about my days in Hollywood.

Ho hum. Truthfully, it was all a bore. The rich and beautiful crowd in Beverly Hills with their gold-plated swimming pools and chauffeured limousines. Bore, bore, bore.

Of course we all thought we were leading interesting lives. But what a lot of rot that was. We were only acting interesting. We were reading words written by other people. How anyone managed to confuse those clever roles and witty lines with our own dull lives will always be a mystery to me.

But never mind that. I MUST think of something to write. I must finish this autobiography since I've already spent the advance money on my new privacy fence and security system.

Must concentrate on my livfe, my lifve, my lifver. (My lifver?) Ah, yes. I must give Madame one of her favorite liver treats. The poor dear is absolutely distressed by this hotel, especially the tiger prints in this room. This must be a cruel joke–a nasty reminder of that inane film I made called "The Tigress of Toledo." Bah! I know I have a photo here somewhere of that worthless piece of celluloid. Ah yes. Here it is.

The studio sent me to the premiere in a tiger-striped Rolls-Royce. Such silliness! I must've received 100 dozen tiger lilies that night. Poo! Flowers are for dead people and piano teachers. And computers are for .... the birdssssssssssss!

DELIVER TO: TYLE DRY CLEANERS
RETURN TO: THE MENAGERIE HOTEL
GUEST NAME: ANNA CONDA, ROOM 401
DATE SENT: THURSDAY, OCTOBER 5
TIME SENT: 10:15 P.M.
PRIORITY: *Return when convenient*

Rhett,

The plant is ravishing. But really, you must be careful. The bailiff asked who it was from and how the sender knew I was here.

Remember, darling, this is all supposed to be a big secret. So please, no more gifts—until the trial is over, that is.

I don't want to hurt your feelings, Rhetty, but so far I'm actually enjoying being sequestered. (You know how I need my personal space.) I've been spending my free time sketching new designs for the spring line of fashions. What do you think?

Anna

P.S. Don't forget to feed our inventory. I'll need lots of skinsssss for these designsssss.

OCTOBUR 5

I WISH I WAS HOME STED OF IN THIS JELL. THE ONLEY GOOD THING IS IVE MAID FREIDNS HERE WITH SUM OF THE RATS WHO LIVE IN THIS JELL. THEYRE NOT AS PURTY AS MY DOGS BUT THEIR NISE AND TAME.

I LIKE RATS. IT ALWEYS MAID ME SAD TO SEE WHAT MISTER TYLE DID WITH THE RATS AT THE ZOO. IM TRYIN NOT TO THINK ABOUT THET NOW. ITS JEST TOO SAID.

HED ANOTHUR CHEESE SANDWIDGE FUR DINUR TUNITE. I RECKON THATS OK. I AINT GOIN TO STERT COMPLAYNING ABOUT THE FOD HERE. IM TRYING TO BE AS GOOD AS I KEN SO MEYBE SUMONE WILL BELIEVE I DIDNT KILL PERRY. SEEMS LIKE PEEPUL DONT TREST ME TO GOOD. I NEVER BEN ABEL TO FIGER OUT WHY.

THE TRYAL BEGINS TOOMOORO. ILL BE HEPPY WHEN ITS ALL OVUR.

LILY WATSON'S JOURNAL
AND

last minute

RESEARCH PAPER

PART TWO

The Trial Begins

This is a sketch by Leon.
He gave me art lessons, but he still draws 500x better than me.

THE MENAGERIE HOTEL
Tyleville, Missouri
A Tyle Entertainment Property

NAME: Lily A. Watson

GRADE: 6

TEACHER: Mr. Holmes

JOURNAL ENTRY FOR: Friday, October 6, during lunch recess

(Excuse the crumbs. I'm eating an egg salad sandwich & chips while I write.)

Today's the first day I really feel like a juror. The bailiff (he's kind of like a guard for us) knocked on all our doors at 6 o'clock this morning and told us to meet at the elevator at 7:00. But I was already awake. I didn't sleep very well last night. I must've turned the air conditioner up too high. When I woke up this morning at 5 o'clock, I could've sworn it was snowing in here!

I turned the a/c down, but couldn't fall back asleep. So I got up, took a shower, and got dressed. Dress pants + blue sweater. (My mom said I couldn't wear jeans to court.) I put my hair in a ponytail and pushed hard on my teeth for a few minutes. I do these teeth exercises every morning and every night to try to straighten them. They're starting to twist in front. If my teeth don't straighten out by next year, my parents say I have to get braces. (Sometimes I swear they're trying to ruin my life.)

After my teeth exercises, I spent 45 minutes practicing walking on my hands. This is something we do in P.E. class and at recess. Not to brag, but I'm probably the best in sixth grade. I learned how to do it in fourth grade because I read in a magazine that walking on your hands prevents pimples. Something about reversing the flow of gravity to your face breaks up pimples before they can form.

I'm only telling you these beauty secrets because I know you're not even reading this journal. I learned a long time ago that the longer an assignment is, the less chance a teacher will actually read it. I could write anything in blah this blah journal blah and you'd probably never even notice. Don't be so sure.

Speaking of noticing, here's something I didn't notice at first: There's no TV in my hotel room. No telephone, either. At breakfast this morning (I had blueberry pancakes and chocolate milk), I sat next to Leon the artist. I asked if he had a TV or telephone in his room. He doesn't either. He said the reason is we're not supposed to have any contact with the outside world.

Supposedly this trial is going to be on the news a lot. Leon said the judge and the lawyers don't want us to hear anything that would make us think Bob White is or isn't guilty. Our decision is supposed to be based on what we see and hear at the trial, not on TV or in newspapers. We can read parts of the newspaper, like the comics and sports. But they'll cut out any articles about the trial.

Still, no TV or telephone??? I also found out we can't swim in the hotel pools OR order room service. We have to do everything in a group so they can keep tabs on us. (Sheesh.) I asked Leon what in the world we're supposed to do at night. He said he'd be happy to give all the jurors painting lessons, which might be fun.

After breakfast, all the jurors piled into a bus. The bailiff drove us over to the courthouse. We had to be in the jury box by 7:55 a.m. because our working day starts at 8 o'clock on the dot.

Outside the courthouse, people were carrying signs and marching against the juvenile juror law. That's me they're talking about! I recognized the woman who was leading the marchers. Her name is Lynn Goe. She was my Girl Scout leader in fourth grade. She's one of those adults who always **hovers** over you when you're trying to do something. We called her Mrs. Goe Away.

Once, during a cookie drive, she made us go door-to-door in groups of five to sell cookies because she thought it was safer that way. *Wrong-Goe.* We nearly killed each other at every house because people always buy exactly 3 boxes of cookies, so it created a big huge fight among the Scouts.

Anyway, I don't think Mrs. Goe recognized me. Even if she did, she wouldn't remember me. I was in Scouts three years and she never learned my name. She called me Millie. I just kept my head down and walked right by her into the courthouse.

When we got inside, a lady showed us where to sit. We all have numbers—juror 1, juror 2, juror 3, etc. I'm juror 12, so I sit in the 12th seat of the jury box, which is the farthest seat on the right in the second row. I don't mind being in the back. I still have a good view of everything. I sit next to Anna Conda and behind Sy Meese, the tuna guy.

The lawyers were already in the courtroom when we got there. Golden Ray Treevor and Mally Mute sat at separate tables facing the high platform where the judge sits. Both lawyers had their briefcases on the tables and they looked really serious.

I counted about 60 people in the courtroom, including Perry's mom and dad. They looked awful and old—like grandparents instead of parents. The Keets used to run a restaurant in town called Keets' Kitchen, but they closed it after Perry died. My mom said Mr. and Mrs. Keet were just too sad to keep the restaurant going.

Looking at them in the courtroom, I believed it. Mr. Keet had his mouth closed real tight, like if he said anything it would be terrible, so he just kept quiet. Mrs. Keet's eyes were all red with big bags underneath them, like she's been crying for months. I feel so bad for her. Perry was an only child, like me.

When Perry and I were in that play together in second grade, I used to go over to the Keets' house all the time so Perry and I could practice our parts—and plan our wedding. *(I hate remembering embarrassing stuff like this.)* Mrs. Keet helped us with our lines and always made great snacks for us, like popcorn balls and brownies. I don't know if I ever thanked her.

Now that I think about it, I owe Mrs. Keet a big apology. When Perry and I were practicing for *Hansel and Gretel,* we made a trail of brownie crumbs all through the Keets' house, just like the characters do in the story. What a mess! But I don't think Mrs. Keet even got mad at us. (My mom would've gone nuts!) Maybe after the trial, I'll write Mrs. Keet a letter and tell her how sorry I am about the brownie crumbs and Perry.

I haven't seen the Keets since Perry's funeral in August. Everybody in town went to it. Since they never found Perry's body, his parents put framed pictures of him on a table, which I thought was 1/2 nice and 1/2 **creepy.**

I went to the funeral with my mom and dad. I had to keep biting my hand so I wouldn't cry, which would've been a complete disaster because everybody in our class was there. Perry was in the most popular group at school. I'm in the second-most popular group. All through the funeral, I kept thinking, *What if I died? Who would come to my funeral?* Then I felt completely guilty for thinking about me instead of Perry.

When we left the church after the funeral, I stubbed my toe on the sidewalk (I was wearing my yellow open-toe sandals) and started crying. To tell you the truth, I was probably crying more about Perry than about my toe, but it was a good excuse.

Whoops. The bailiff just told us our lunch break is over. Gotta finish this sandwich and get back to work. I'll write more (and better) tonight.

The Tyleville Quill

Tyle Publishing
Rhett Tyle, Publisher

50 cents................................Friday, October 6.....................Morning Edition

Opening statements scheduled in Bob White trial

Opening statements in the Bob White trial are scheduled to begin today.

Prosecutor Golden Ray Treevor will address the jury first. Treevor intends to prove beyond a reasonable doubt that Bob White murdered 11-year-old Perry Keet and then disposed of the body.

The prosecution's chief witness will be Rhett Tyle, owner of Tyle Park Zoo. Tyle is expected to testify that Bob White made references to killing Perry Keet, which were later confirmed in a confession signed by White.

Court-appointed public defender Mallory Mute will represent Bob White. The trial is expected to last one month.

White (l) will be represented by Mute (r)

Treevor (r) will ask Tyle (l) to testify

Priscilla the gorilla declared National Treasure

WASHINGTON, D.C.–In a ceremony held yesterday in the White House Rose Garden, President Lee Myrrh declared Priscilla the gorilla a National Treasure.

"Priscilla's paintings remind us all of the importance of both art and animals in our daily lives," said President Lee Myrrh, who called Priscilla "a fine American."

World-famous inventor and entertainer Rhett Tyle traveled by private jet to Washington to accept the award on behalf of Priscilla, who remains on display in Tyle Park Zoo in Tyleville, Mo.

Rhett Tyle made headlines a decade ago with his famous Snake-in-a-Cake invention, which became a national craze before it was outlawed by health officials. Earlier in his career, Tyle invented and patented a motorized hot air balloon called the Tyle-malloon. He settled in Missouri nine years ago, after his Tyle-malloon veered off course during a tornado.

Rhett Tyle accepts award for Priscilla

Tyle's wacky inventions made him a billionaire

Did you know that gorillas . . .

❏ are primates
❏ are vegetarian
❏ are known as "great apes" (so are orangutans and chimpanzees)
❏ are called the "gentle giants"
❏ are diurnal (that means they build their nests in a different location each night)
❏ have individual "noseprints" much like human fingerprints
❏ often beat their chests when excited or alarmed
❏ are highly intelligent

What's the Buzz

by

Bernie "Buzz" Ard

Parlay-voo jury duty? Me neither. But here are a couple of terms I've got to keep in mind, and you should, too, if you're playing along at home.

Prosecution: That's the side pointing a finger at the defendant, saying he's (or she's) guilty of a crime. In this case, it's the State of Missouri, acting on the behalf of its citizens.

Defendant: A person, like Bob White, charged with a crime.

Jury: A group of 12 ordinary citizens (like *moi*) who must decide whether a defendant is guilty or not guilty.

Evidence: Testimony from witnesses, documents, and other stuff.

Oath: A promise to tell the truth, the whole truth, and nothing but the truth.

Witness: A person who tells the court what he or she knows about the case.

Sequestered: That's when a jury is holed up in a hotel, without TV, radio, or telephones.

But who knew sequestration could be so chichi? This ain't bad, folks. I can't tell you where we're staying, but I'll say this much: It's the finest animal-themed hotel in the world AND a property of Tyle Entertainment. 'Nuff said.

And hold on to your hats for this next item: Guess who I sat next to at last night's get-acquainted dinner? Only the most talented, mysterious, reclusive, retired actress in the solar system. Hint: A fan mag once described her famous eyes as "reminiscent of a tame deer."

But no one ever tamed her. No siree! This box office queen always took pleasure in turning down Hollywood's million-dollar suitors. She's the vixen who told Clark Sable to scram and Beary Grant to beat it. But she could read me the riot act and I wouldn't care.

Seated across from the box office queen was a local artist of some notoriety. (And, no, not Priscilla.) To my left was a collector of pricey fashions, not to mention pricey men.

A delightful 12-year-old sat two chairs down from me. Kudos to the parents of this well-mannered young carrottop!

The remaining jurors include a truck driver, a hairstylist, a schoolteacher, a retired florist, a furniture store owner, and an orthodontist with the annoying habit of telling root canal horror stories at mealtimes. Quite an interesting mix of bipeds, are we not?

Opening arguments begin today. Stay tuned.

"Buzz"

Golden Ray Treevor
Prosecuting Attorney

The State of Missouri vs. Bob White

Witness list for the prosecution

1. Mrs. Eleanor Keet
2. Police Chief Jay Byrd
3. ***Rhett Tyle (STAR WITNESS)***

FROM THE DESK OF MALLORY MUTE
Public Defender
Tyle County, Missouri

Witness list for the defense

1. Bob White
2.
3.
4.
5.
6.
7.
8.
9.
10.

THE MENAGERIE HOTEL

Tyleville, Missouri

A Tyle Entertainment Property

NAME: Lily A. Watson

GRADE: 6

TEACHER: Mr. Holmes

JOURNAL ENTRY FOR: Friday, October 6, 9:45 p.m.

Just got back from dinner. We ate at Moo Goo Gi Tyle. I had sweet-and-sour chicken. Here's my fortune:

> You are smarter than the serpent and swifter than the eagle.

Whatever that means.

Anyway, back to the trial this morning: All of us jurors were sitting in our assigned seats. Then, at 8 o'clock on the dot it suddenly got dead silent. At first, I couldn't figure out why. Then I looked across the courtroom and saw two guards bringing Bob White into the courtroom.

He was still wearing that same orange jumpsuit, but for some reason he looked creepier than he did the other day during jury selection. Maybe because it suddenly dawned on me that this is **The Real Thing.**

I must've flinched or something when I saw him because Anna Conda, who sits right next to me, squeezed my hand and whispered, "Don't worry, precious. We're safe from that savage here."

At the time I thought it was nice, but now it kind of bugs me. I don't want to be treated any different because I'm the only kid on the jury. I don't want people (like Mrs. Goe Away) thinking they have to protect me from anything I might hear or see.

It was nice and all of Anna to say. And it's nice of Mrs. Goe to think that marching against the juvenile juror law is going to keep kids safe. But the fact is, we're NOT safe. Nobody is. That's the whole point. There's no such thing as being safe—here or anywhere. People get hurt every day. Some people get killed by weirdos like Bob White and some people just get teased to death at the lunch table for drinking orange soda or eating a tuna fish sandwich.

I didn't tell you this earlier, but the reason I know not to bring tuna for lunch is because when I was in third grade I brought a tuna salad sandwich in my lunch box. I was called "Little Friskies Breath" for a year! And the one and ONLY time I ever bought orange soda at school, the boys in my class told everyone not to drink it or they'd end up with orange hair like me. (Also, remember before when I said I was in the second-most popular group? Really, I'm in the third-most popular group.)

I'm rambling because I'm tired. It was a long day. And we really didn't hear anything about Bob White or Perry Keet. The judge made us leave so he could listen to the lawyers argue over some nitpicky stuff.

Almost forgot to tell you about the judge! His name is E. Gall. He's bald and wears a long black robe. I thought that was just on TV. It's cool, in a corny way.

Some of the jurors are not so cool. There's one lady named Sandy Piper. She's a teacher at the private school in town. Every day she wears these big dopey pins on her blouses, like ladybugs and unicorns.

My grandma used to call those kind of pins "brooches." I always called them roaches. Anyway, Mrs. Piper tried to get us all to sing "Row, Row, Row Your Boat" as a round this morning on the way to the courthouse. She said she was going to grade us! Teachers never quit, do they? She also chews too loud and always wants me to play boring old card games with her and some of the other *groan-ups*.

I'm not crazy about juror 5 either. His name is Dr. L. E. Font and he's a dentist who does braces (an orthoblahblahblah, or however you spell it). He's the same guy who was whistling and flossing those first days of jury selection. Dr. Font has these looooooong sideburns and he wears his hair in a big floofy pompadour. Of course when he saw my teeth, he asked when I'm getting braces. I felt like asking when he was getting an earthling haircut.

There's also a beautician on the jury. Her name's Kim Illion. Every night after dinner she asks me if she can trim my bangs. ARGH! Why do adults feel like they have to FIX you all day long? It drives me crazy. I feel like I'm being held hostage by these people.

Once when my parents and I went to Chicago, they were driving me completely nuts. So I wrote "HELP! I'M BEING HELD HOSTAGE BY THESE CRAZY PEOPLE!" on the back of a notebook and held it up in the back window of the car. Nobody did anything but wave. One guy even gave me the thumbs-up, which was totally insulting.

Fawn Papillon is my favorite juror, even though she's really old. I sat across from her at dinner tonight. I think she could tell I like her little dog because she asked if I wanted to "take a constitutional" with them tomorrow morning at 6 o'clock. I told her I took the Constitution test last year and got an A minus on it. She laughed and said she meant would I like to take a walk with her and her dog tomorrow morning. ("Constitutional" also means walk, if you can believe that.) I told Fawn yes.

I'm too tired to push my teeth back tonight. I'll do my antibraces exercises twice as long tomorrow. Here's a treat for you, Mr. Holmes, for reading this blah blah blah journal. (The stripes on this zebra are white and dark chocolate!) Give me a sign if you really are reading this.

Thank you.

MY AUTOBIOGRAPHY
BY
FAWN PAPILLON

Saturday night

No jury duty today or tomorrow, so there's no excuse for not buckling down and getting at least one chapter under my belt.

First things first.

CHAPTER ONE: MY YOUTH

~~When I was young~~
~~As a young girl~~
~~When I was younger, I~~

Achthpfllaat! It's been 70-some years since I was a young girl. How in blazes am I supposed to remember my early days?

I can't even recall what I looked like back then. Average height, I think. A little on the skinny side. Red hair and crooked teeth, which were promptly capped and straightened as soon as I got to Hollywood. I must have a photo somewhere in this box. Ah yes, here we are.

Oh, for goodness sake! That's it. Lily! No wonder I like that little rascal across the hall. With her tomboy style and lopsided grin, Lily reminds me of my younger self. She even looks like me in my first movie: "Misty: The Moroccan Misfit." They let me use my real name in that film. Fanny Pigeon. Ha! I'd almost forgotten about that.

But, goodness, that was decades ago, before I got caught

65

up in the madness of Hollywood and became a prisoner of fame, unable to walk down the street or drive a car because of all the cameras and reporters.

People say I became bitter. Maybe I did. But all I ever wanted was my freedom. The newspapers said I abandoned my fans. I didn't. I was trapped by my circumstances, like that poor man in jail. Like a bird in a cage. Like the birds in this hotel. Like–

Oh, gravy stains! Now I AM sounding like a bitter old windbag. What would Fanny Pigeon think about that? Ho, ho. A piece of chocolate to soothe my nerves and then to bed. I haven't seen the evening news since I left my compound. Wonder who the jackals in the media are stalking this week.

K-TYLE FM 100
TyleRadio for Tyleville
Transcript
Monday, October 9

KEN AIRY: From the majestic studios of K-TYLE atop Tyle-O-Tropolis in downtown Tyleville, this is Ken Airy with K-TYLE news on the hour. Our top story tonight is Bob White on trial for his life. K-TYLE TV reporter Maggie Pie has spent the day at the Tyle County Courthouse. Maggie, what can you tell us?

MAGGIE PIE: Well, Ken, things are getting off to a slow start in the case of the State of Missouri versus Bob White. Opening statements, scheduled to begin on Friday, have been delayed at least one more day while attorneys and the judge set ground rules for the trial. Attorneys spent most of today debating two issues: First, whether jurors will be allowed to take notes during the trial and second, whether cameras will be allowed in the court-room.

KEN AIRY: What was the outcome?

MAGGIE PIE: On the question of note taking, Judge F. Gall said he did not anticipate there would be sufficient technical evidence to merit it, meaning jurors will not be able to take notes during the trial. And as for cam-eras in the courtroom, the judge echoed the words of the defense in saying he did not want this trial to become a media circus.

KEN AIRY: So we won't have televised coverage of the trial?

MAGGIE PIE: No, but listeners will be able to hear gavel-to-gavel coverage of the trial right here on K-TYLE FM 100. And readers of *The Tyleville Quill* will be able to see sketches of the trial drawn by a court illustrator, who will be permitted in the courtroom each day to sketch her impressions of the trial.

KEN AIRY: Speaking of artistic impressions, we're hearing reports that Priscilla the gorilla has painted two new canvases that are creating quite a buzz.

MAGGIE PIE: That's right. In fact, I'm jumping in a Tyle Taxi right this minute and dashing over to the zoo with my Tyle-Cam so our K-TYLE TV subscribers can see a live satellite feed of the paintings that have art critics scratching their heads.

The Tyleville Quill

Tyle Publishing
Rhett Tyle, Publisher

50 cents.....................Tuesday, October 10..................Morning Edition

Priscilla's new paintings have critics going bananas

Priscilla's latest paintings at Tyle Park Zoo

Could this be Priscilla's "Blue Period"?

Two new canvases were discovered late yesterday in the cage-turned-gallery of Priscilla, the celebrated gorilla at Tyle Park Zoo.

While Priscilla has produced countless paintings since her creative inspiration began in August, these latest paintings represent a departure from her earlier abstract works, which were more playful and colorful.

When asked to explain the significance of the new paintings, zoo owner Rhett Tyle responded with several questions of his own.

"What do these new paintings mean?" Tyle asked. "How the pickled Picasso should I know? Priscilla's a genius. That's what it means. We've got offers coming in from Hong Kong to Helsinki for these paintings."

But according to some art critics, the new paintings reflect a darker, more surreal mood for the gorilla.

"I find Priscilla's new paintings deeply disturbing," said Dr. Art X. Spurt, a professor of art history at Tyle University. "It's clear to me that Priscilla is struggling to express her inner gorilla angst through the use of these brooding colors and textures."

When asked if he was bothered by critics who find the sudden switch in styles troubling, Rhett Tyle replied: "Critics schmitics. Do they ever buy art? That's what I want to know. I'm talking to art dealers who are ready to pony up $1 million for just one of Priscilla's paintings. I think I'll listen to their opinions instead of these fancy-pants critics with their Ph.D.'s who don't give a tarantula's turd about priceless works of modern art."

(Publisher's note: Effective tomorrow, Dr. Art X. Spurt is no longer employed by Tyle University.)

What's the Buzz

by

Bernie "Buzz" Ard

From the trenches:

Rumor has it the prosecution's chief witness in the White trial will be Rhett Tyle. I know Tyle, of course. He's my boss at the paper. And whatta boss! Hates my column. Never reads it. He inherited me when he blew into town (literally) nine years ago and bought this paper.

And if I had a nickel for every time Tyle told me that he lines the cages in the zoo with my column . . . fuggetaboudit. But that's Tyle for you. He's the guy who bills himself as Tyleville's First Tycoon. What's a tycoon anyway? Sounds like a cross between a tiger and a toucan.

Well, Rhett has a large bill anyway. Make that large bills. Big bucks.

It's a thrice-told tale by now how he made a fortune off his wacky invention. You remember it, of course: Snake-in-a-Cake. One out of every 100 cakes had a real live rat snake baked right in it. Charming, eh? But they sold like hotcakes. Or was it hot snakes? What a craze! What a fad!

No deaths were reported from Snake-in-a-Cake, but imagine the one in 100 who got the snake. (Wonder if it tasted like chicken?) The craze ended when the feds got Tyle on a cruelty-to-animals rap. I could never figure if it was cruelty to snakes or to us Homo sapiens.

Well, Tyle got stuck holding the bag–of snakes, that is. You know the rest of the story. He settled in our town and started a bazillion businesses. Since then, the old snake handler's become a Tyleville legend in his own mind and quite the foolanthropist, starting up crazy enterprises like that half-baked zoo.

Leave it to smooth-as-snake-oil Tyle

to turn it into a sideshow with that art-loving gorilla of his. You've seen Tyle's new license plates, haven't you? IMAPE4ART. Geddit? Gottit. Tyle's a wheeler-dealer, all right. A real glad-hander, if you can hang onto his oily hand. Oh yeah, and he likes the ladies. (Sorry, juror 11!)

I've been trying to get an interview with Tyle for nine years. Always says he doesn't have time. Then he turns around and has a regular gabfest with anyone holding a TV camera, especially if "anyone" happens to be of the female persuasion.

But there's more to life than getting the celeb interview. Like death, for instance. Which is what this case is all about. Let's not forget that.

"Buzz"

THE MENAGERIE HOTEL
OUTGOING LAUNDRY

DELIVER TO: TYLE DRY CLEANERS
RETURN TO: THE MENAGERIE HOTEL
GUEST NAME: ANNA CONDA, ROOM 401
DATE SENT: TUESDAY, OCTOBER 10
TIME SENT: 8:15 P.M.
PRIORITY: *Please return clothes ASAP*

Rhett,

I'm worried about the new paintings. Why the sudden change in styles? I don't want to ruin a good thing by taking unnecessary risks.

Perhaps you could persuade Priscilla to cease and desist. Or at least scale back.

Scale back? Oh, my word. Inspiration!

Scales are back! Come to House of S-Tyle Fashions for the latest designs in exotic leathers

It's astonishing how sequestration is feeding my creativity. Perhaps it's like a much-needed hibernation.

Now go take care of Priscilla, sweet dreams.

Ssssssssincerely,
Anna

71

51243

Tyle Dry Cleaners

Sp●ts, Stains and Wrinkles Removed with a Twinkle
Here are your clothes—cleaned to perfection!

PLEASE DELIVER TO:	LAUNDRY RETURNED:
ANNA CONDA ROOM 401, The Menagerie Hotel Tyle-O-Tropolis	9:14 P.M.

Anna,

I'm not crazy about the new paintings either. You know I don't like this modern art crud. But the public loves it! There's a stooge born every minute.

I'm getting phone calls from art dealers all over the globe. Everybody wants to get his paws on a Priscilla original. I just got off the horn with a dealer from New York who's ready to pay ONE million clams for one of the chump's paintings. Ha! Never underestimate the power of a good freak show. Catch their eye, then make 'em buy!

So here's what I'm thinking. What if we held an art auction? We could sell some of these doodles to the highest bidders and make a killing. Then we'd make a clean break. Going, going, GONE!

Just thinking out loud here. What do you say?

I keep forgetting to tell you there's a fire escape right outside your hotel window. Could be useful for private meetings, if Ms. Cold-Blooded will allow me to invade her personal space sometime.

Back to the scales,

Rhett

One-hour service guaranteed with a smile . . . or my name isn't Tyle!

OUTGOING LAUNDRY

DELIVER TO: TYLE DRY CLEANERS
RETURN TO: THE MENAGERIE HOTEL
GUEST NAME: ANNA CONDA, ROOM 401
DATE SENT: TUESDAY, OCTOBER 10
TIME SENT: 10 P.M.
PRIORITY: *Take your time, dear*

Rhett,

One MILLION dollars? Darling, that's sensational. If we play our cards right, we'll have enough Priscilla originals to make $100 million!

I adore the idea of an art auction. It's the perfect venue for our departure. (Going, going, gone, indeed!) Then we could take this show on the road. How about another world tour? Remember how successful the last one was?

This time Priscilla's paintings would be our main attraction. We could hit Europe, the Far East, Australia. Just think of the $$$ we'd make selling the chump's artwork. And I could sell some of my designer fashions during the tour.

This show has just begun! Start working on the publicity. I'll look for details in the paper. You're a genius!

*Your favorite **warm-blooded** juror.*   *XO*

Anna

P.S. Come visit anytime.

<u>People who know</u>:

✓ 1. Me - OK

✓ 2. Anna - OK

(almost)✓ 3. Bob White - headed for the Slammer - OK

 4. The Chump - Take on tour with Anna & me?

  - 2 risks.

  - Better get rid of b4 we leave. How?

  - Need to think about that.

  - Also need more paintings for tour.

Need to order

For the chump -
canvas
paint
frames
bananas

For me -
tux
mustache wax
teeth whitener
eye drops

When to hold art auction?

Trial began .   Oct. 6

Trial supposed
       to last   +4 weeks =

Should end ———→ Nov 3

Art Auction = Nov 4?

                     Saturday.

                     Perfect!

Interview tomorrow with
       Maggie Pie

Things to remember during
interview:
- Sit up straight
- Don't use ~~the~~ any
    sloppy grammar
- Wink at camera?
- Talk about Priscilla—
              A LOT!

- Keep mum about
    Anna
- If reporter asks about
    the kid, cry croc. tears

THE MAGGIE PIE SPECIAL
A Production of K-TYLE TV

An Up Close and Intimate Interview with . . .

RHETT TYLE

MAGGIE PIE: You've seen his name in the headlines. His zoo is the talk of the nation. And in a few short days, he'll be the prosecution's chief witness in the Bob White trial. But who is the man behind the headlines? Who is Rhett Tyle? We decided to visit the penthouse offices of Tyle Enterprises to find out what makes this man tick.

(Music plays during opening montage of Tyle as a child.)

Rhett A. Tyle was born in a small town in Oklahoma. He grew up in a family of circus performers. His act? Snake charming. But he left the carnival when his ingenious Snake-in-a-Cake invention made him an overnight billionaire. Nine years ago Rhett arrived in town by accident when his Tyle-malloon veered off course during a violent tornado. But he liked what he saw here and decided to stay. Since then he single-handedly has transformed our one-stop-sign town into a thriving metropolis. Make that a Tyle-O-Tropolis, the most ambitious entertainment center ever built. In its first year of operation, Tyle-O-Tropolis was named the number one tourist attraction in the Midwest. Tyle's empire now occupies 97 percent of the property in Tyleville and accounts for 100 percent of the town's employment. Last year, residents in his adopted hometown honored Tyle by voting to rename our county and city after him in appreciation of all he's

76

given to this community. One of Rhett's many civic contributions is Tyle Park Zoo, which this year has been a source of both sorrow and joy for multibillionaire Rhett Tyle.

MAGGIE PIE: Mr. Tyle, it's been quite a year for you. First, a child was murdered at your zoo, allegedly by one of your employees. Then, just a few weeks later, a gorilla starts creating priceless works of art in her cage. How have you dealt with the roller coaster of emotions?

RHETT TYLE: Heck, I love roller coasters, so that hasn't been no . . . er . . . any problem.

MAGGIE PIE: You love roller coasters, do you? Hmmmm . . . How very interesting. What is it about them that you love? And why?

RHETT TYLE: Well, that's easy. I grew up in the carnival. My daddy was the tall man. My mama was the fat woman. And me, I was their tall, fat baby! Heck, I learned to walk on the tightrope.

MAGGIE PIE: What was it like for you, growing up in the carnival? Did the children at school tease you?

RHETT TYLE: School? Lady, you got the wrong pony. I didn't go to any school. Everything I know I learned from the carnies. They taught me how to pull rabbits out of top hats and Easter bonnets. How to charm snakes. How to work without a net. How to escape from locked vaults, straitjackets, sealed rooms, frosted cakes, even a Turkish jail cell.

MAGGIE PIE: Sounds like quite an education.

RHETT TYLE (winking at camera): You bet your circus peanuts it was!

MAGGIE PIE: Was it during your years with the carnival that you developed your love for animals?

RHETT TYLE: Yes, indeedy. I'm an old softie when it comes to animals. Show me a basket of fluffy kittens and I cry like a baby. Zookeepers in other cities tell me I treat the animals at Tyle Park Zoo too well. They say my animals live like kings. Well, I can't help myself. I like to think of my zoo as a hotel for animals. Nothing but the best for our zoo guests!

MAGGIE PIE: No wonder you were recently named "Tyleville Humanitarian and Animalitarian of the Year." Getting back to your early years, what other life lessons did you learn from your days in the carnival?

RHETT TYLE: First thing you learn in the carnival is don't believe everything you see. But the next lesson is even more important: Don't believe everything you think. Ha! Now there's a secret for you. That's how I became the Great Tylini, Master of Illusion. (Tyle gestures to wall.)

MAGGIE PIE: Is that you on that poster?

(Close-up of carnival poster hanging in Tyle's office.)

RHETT TYLE: Darn right it's me. Quite the Romeo, eh?

MAGGIE PIE: Yes, indeed. And that brings me to my next question. Romance. Love. Passion. Is there someone in your life -- a Juliet, perhaps -- who provides that kind of magic for you?

RHETT TYLE: Well, shoot! I didn't know you were going to ask snoopy questions like that.

MAGGIE PIE: People can't help wondering about the personal lives of the rich and famous. Tell us, Mr. Tyle. Is there a special someone in your life?

RHETT TYLE: Showman's privilege prevents me from disclosing the particulars of my personal life. Remember, I am a man of mystery.

MAGGIE PIE: Rumor has it you've been courting a certain fashion plate named Anna Con --

RHETT TYLE: Aw, conundrum! I can't tell a lie. Of course there's a little lady in my life! And her name is . . . uh . . . her name's Priscilla! The princess of primates! The thinking-man's gorilla! This old gal's creating priceless, one-of-a-kind masterpieces. You won't find art like this just anywhere. No siree! We're talking exotic, hypnotic, macrobiotic works of art. Right here in Tyleville, the gorilla art capital of the world!

MAGGIE PIE: Getting back to --

RHETT TYLE: Priscilla! And how about the Priscilla Parade and Art Auction? It's right around the corner. Saturday, November fourth. Mark your calendar today!

OCTOBUR 11

SO FAR THIS TRYAL ISENT AS BED AS I THAWT IT WOOD
BE. MOSTLY I JEST SIT THER AND LISSEN TO THE LAYURS
TALK.

THE WAY IT WERKS IS IT REELLY DONT MATTUR WHAT THE
LAYURS THINCK. ITS ALL UP TO THE JURURS. THERE THE
WONS WHO HAVE TO DUSIDE WETHER I DID IT OR NOT.

TODAY I TRYED LOOKIN OVER AT THEM JURURS AND SMILLIN
JEST A LITTUL BIT TO SHO THEM I AINT AS BAD AS
EVURYONE THINCKS. NOBUDY SMILLED BACK AT ME. EGSEP
ONE GIRL WHO LOOCKED ABOUT PERRYS ADGE. I LIKED
TO WAVE AT HER BUT I DINDT THINCK IDDID BE RITE TO
WAVE IN COORT. SHE SMILLED AT ME FUR ONE SECKOND
AND THEN LOOKT DOWN.

I DONT NO WHAT SHES DOIN OVER THERE WITH ALL THEM
ADULTS BUT IM GLAD THERES ONE NICE PURHSON THERE. IM
NOT SO GOOD WITH PEEPUL BUT THE RATS IN THIS JELL SURE
LIKE ME. I WISH A CUPLE OF THEM WAS ON THE JURY.

IT JEST STARTID RANEING OUTSIDE. I ALWEYS LIKED TO
LISSEN TO THE RANE ON MY TIN RUF AT HOME. RANE
SOWNDS DIFRUNT WEN YURE IN JELL. EVRYTHING IS DIFRUNT
WHEN YURE IN JELL. BUT IM TRYING NOT TO FEEL TO SAD
FUR MYSALF BECAWS AT LEEST IM ALIVE AND NOT DED
LIKE POOR PERRY.

MY AUTOBIOGRAPHY
BY
FAWN PAPILLON

CHAPTER ONE
Wednesday night

Rainy today. Dreary inside and out. Was there ever such a gloomy time of year? I suppose the month I spent in Paris filming "Love Me? Oui, Oui!" was worse. Oh, how I felt like flinging myself down that grand staircase! Surely I have a photo from that silly movie.

And why in thunder did I think I'd get any work done on my autobiography during this trial? It's much too grisly. The death of a child . . . A simple-minded man blamed for it . . . Good heavens. It's too sad for words.

And my poor Madame is at wit's end. The birds in this hotel torment her. It's not their fault, of course. Captivity makes them mean. Seeing those poor birds in their golden cages makes me think of my own gilded prison. How many times have I felt like a bird with clipped wings?

Oh, nuts. Enough with the melodrama, Fanny. Guess I'm in a soupy mood tonight. There's a strange melancholy to this hotel. And to this whole trial. Wish I could put my finger on what it is that haunts my sad thoughts.

Maybe I'm just blue like the gorilla in the zoo. That poor creature. Another artist in a cage. And people wonder why she paints such brooding pictures?

At least it's quiet here. Perfect conditions for writing. Now if only I could think of something to write. But how can I author a book when I haven't even authored a life?

Oh, bah. Pass the chocolates.

What's the Buzz
by
Bernie "Buzz" Ard

Here's an interesting parlor game.

Take 14 people to a courthouse at eight o'clock in the ayem. Shuffle them in and out of the courtroom all morning. Feed them greasy fish sandwiches and coleslaw for lunch. More shuffling in the afternoon. Give them an hour of free time to relax–without TV or radio.

Then, sit them around a dinner table in the back room of a no-star restaurant and forbid them to talk about the events of the day.

Unbearable? You got that right.

The good news is we have in our midst a screen legend who probably has more tales to tell than all of us combined.

The bad news is the movie queen is modest to a fault. This rare bird won't tell us word one about her days in Hollywood. Drat! And this, you'll recall, is the eccentric starlet who once had an authentic French guillotine delivered to a pain-in-the-neck studio exec with a one-word note: "Cut!"

But it's fun to see our movie star (juror 2) enjoying the company of the youngest member of the jury (juror 12). Despite the 70-year age gap, the two are becoming fast friends. I must tell you, juror 12 has almost as much style as our living legend.

In the courtroom, our junior juror looks and acts like a perfect young lady. But back here in the hotel, she's usually seen sporting a T-shirt, baggy shorts, green fingernail polish, and a baseball cap–worn backward, of course–over her pumpkin-colored tresses.

The cap comes off only when she's walking on her hands down the fourth floor hallway, a trick she's famous for among her fellow sixth graders at Tyleville Middle School. Now she says she's determined to teach me.

Jurors 7, 8, 9, and 10 spend most of their off-hours playing cards. Juror 5, our resident orthodontist, lectured the group last night on the importance of dental hygiene. He even shared with us his favorite video, *Flossing Is Fun!* There's one in every crowd, isn't there?

From the Oops! department: Seems I offended juror 11 with an item in a recent column when I mentioned a certain shade of lipstick seen on a certain gentleman's collar.

Hey, I call 'em as I see 'em. Besides, some people should just loosen their flea collars and relax a little. And, anyway, my mission is to ruffle as many feathers as possible–to met mixaphors.

Gotta run. Juror 12 says I must practice walking on my hands.

Upside-downly yours,

"Buzz"

NAME: Lily A. Watson

GRADE: 6

TEACHER: Mr. Holmes

JOURNAL ENTRY FOR: Thursday, October 12, 10:15 p.m.

Guess what I did this morning before breakfast? I took a "constitutional" with Fawn Papillon. I've been taking them with her all week. Oh, and I found out what kind of dog Madame is: a papillon. It's a breed of toy spaniel from Europe.

"Papillon" is the French word for "butterfly," which is what Madame's ears are shaped like. Fawn says papillons were really popular with empresses and queens way back whenever.

When Fawn and I first started taking our constitutionals, we planned to walk Madame outside, around Tyle-O-Tropolis. Problem was the bailiff heard us in the hallway and told us we couldn't leave the hotel. Not even to walk a dog! We told him we wouldn't buy a newspaper or watch TV or anything, but he said no way. So we have to walk Madame up and down the fourth floor hallway of the hotel instead.

It turns out the bailiff could lose his job if somebody saw us outside during sequestration. Besides, Fawn said Madame could just as well "do her business" in her bathroom. Fawn also said if I wanted, Madame could spend the night in my room some night, which would be GREAT. I wonder if she was serious.

During this morning's walk, Fawn told me she named Madame after her favorite opera, *Madame Butterfly.* Then Fawn started prancing up and down the hall, singing these laaa laaaa laaaaaaaaa opera-y songs. We were both laughing like crazy—until Dr. L. E. Font in 408 opened his door and asked us if we could please **"pipe down."**

The only problem was Dr. Font was wearing these pajamas that had dancing teeth all over them. Fawn took one look at him and shrieked **"Holy molars!"** and we both fell on the floor laughing.

Fawn is so much fun. I can't believe she's 82 years old. When she was my age, she was already a movie star, which makes me feel like a complete zero. Guess what she does first thing every morning? She gives Madame a doggie treat and gives herself a little piece of chocolate. Before breakfast! Fawn says eating chocolate whenever you want is one of the privileges of being old.

I told her about my lunch table at school and some of the rules they have. She scrunched up her nose and said, "Only silly fools care what other people think of them." She also said popularity is for cowards and that she doesn't give a "rip" what people think of her.

I love the funny crabby way Fawn talks. And maybe she's right about popularity. But she doesn't know what sixth grade is like. Being popular is a matter of life or death. Maybe it's not that way with teachers, so go ahead and order a tuna sandwich and orange soda if you dare.

(Notice that I'm not going back and crossing anything out, like you said I shouldn't. I'm just changing my mind on some things. I better not get docked points for that, do I?) **No.**

But back to these stupid jury rules: They completely tick me off. It's like being in jail. Why should I have to be locked up like Bob White? I didn't kill anybody.

I really shouldn't gripe. If it weren't for jury duty, I never would've gotten to stay at The Menagerie Hotel and eat in restaurants every morning and night. We went to Rhettalini's last night and I ordered the same thing as Fawn: eggplant Parmesan. Deee-lish! My mom would die if she knew I was eating weird food like this. Still no shrimp cocktail yet.

I wish I could live in a hotel and eat in restaurants forever. If I had a phone and TV, it'd be perfect. The only bad thing is not being able to visit Tyle Park Zoo and see Priscilla's new paintings. I can't believe I'm missing the most exciting thing in Tyleville history.

I thought jury duty would be exciting, but so far the lawyers keep running us in and out of the courtroom so they can talk to the judge behind our back about the rules for the case. It's kind of boring, but it's still ten times better than school. I just hope I'm not getting too far behind.

One subject I know I'm not getting behind in is art. Leon D. Vinci gave us all a painting lesson tonight in his room. He hung a clothesline so the paintings could dry. Since he didn't have enough watercolor paper for all the jurors, I got to paint the sides of his bathtub.

Leon gave me some watercolor paints to take back to my room so I can practice. I think I'll paint something for Robin the housekeeper.

Well, I'd love to keep chatting, Mr. Holmes, but I can't write and do my teeth exercises at the same time. You'll just have to find something else to read.

That reminds me of another thing that burns me about this journal thing: How come I have to do all the work and all you do is sit back and read what I'm writing? Or not read what I'm writing, which is probably more like it. Last year when a sixth grader broke both legs and missed TWO WHOLE MONTHS of school, she didn't have to keep a journal, so I don't see why I should have to. It's just completely dumb to sit here writing this blah blah blah stuff that nobody will ever blah blah read. This is busywork at its worst. At its liverworst! I dare you to read this journal. I double dare and triple dare and truth or dare you to read this.

Challenge accepted.
With pleasure.

THE MENAGERIE HOTEL
Guest Comment Card

Friday, 10/13

Hi, Robin!

Look in the bathtub. I hope you won't get mad. It washes off real easy with water. I'll clean it up if you want me to.

Lily Watson

P.S. Don't forget: It's Friday the 13th! WOOOOoooowoooooooOWoooo. I'm kidding. I don't believe that superstitious junk about ghosts or spirits, do you?

Robin,

Thanks for
keeping my
room so neat!
Lily W.

Friday, 10/13*

Miss Watson,

Your painting brightened my whole day!

It's a shame to wash it off. Why don't you use paper for your future paintings so you can save them? I'll leave an extra folder of hotel stationery on your desk.

And thank YOU for thanking me. It's very kind of you to appreciate my work.

Sincerely,

Robin

Housekeeping Department

P.S. Good luck on jury duty!

*No, I don't pay much attention to superstition either.

K-TYLE FM 100
TyleRadio for Tyleville
Transcript
Friday, October 13

KEN AIRY: Live from the majestic studios of K-TYLE atop Tyle-O-Tropolis in downtown Tyleville, this is Ken Airy with K-TYLE news on the hour. Opening statements finally began today in the Bob White trial with attorneys on opposite sides painting two very different portraits of the defendant. K-TYLE TV reporter Maggie Pie is covering the story. Maggie, what did we learn today about Bob White?

MAGGIE PIE: Well, Ken, it depends which side you believe. According to prosecuting attorney Golden Ray Treevor, Bob White is a cold-blooded killer who murdered young Perry Keet and then disposed of the body.

KEN AIRY: And how did the defense describe White?

MAGGIE PIE: Defense attorney Mally Mute described Bob White as a simple man but not a bad man. Remember, Ken, the defense does not have to prove that White is innocent. Mute spent much of her opening statement reminding the jury that the burden of proof rests with the prosecution. Golden Ray Treevor, representing the State of Missouri, must prove beyond a reasonable doubt that Bob White is guilty.

KEN AIRY: How does it look so far?

MAGGIE PIE: Too early to say, Ken. Today we heard opening statements. Monday we'll hear from the prosecution's first witness, Perry's mother, Eleanor Keet.

KEN AIRY: Thank you, Maggie. And now, on a lighter note: There was big news today at Tyle Park Zoo, where a new painting containing a cryptic message was discovered in Priscilla the gorilla's cage. Spectators marveled at Priscilla's mastery of the English language, but were puzzled by the significance of her words: "LAW Remember Me." Zoo owner Rhett Tyle thought the meaning was obvious.

(CUT TO TAPE OF RHETT TYLE)

RHETT TYLE: Why, it's clear as Christmas. Priscilla's a smart gal. She knows what's going on over at the courthouse. She's asking everyone to remember the rule of law. An eye for an eye. A tooth for a tooth. Bob White is a murderer and that's the truth!

The Tyleville Quill

Tyle Publishing
Rhett Tyle, Publisher

50 cents.................................Saturday, October 14...............Morning Edition

PRISCILLA CAN WRITE!
Tyleville's amazing gorilla makes opening statement

Priscilla the gorilla displays her latest painting

If you thought Priscilla's paintings were impressive, hold on to your hat. It now appears the nation's favorite gorilla can also write.

What's more, the gentle giant has chosen a dramatic moment to write what by all accounts is an impassioned plea for justice.

"LAW Remember Me" were the words painted in bold colors on a canvas discovered yesterday in Priscilla's cage at the Tyle Park Zoo.

Opening statements made in Bob White trial

THE MENAGERIE HOTEL
OUTGOING LAUNDRY

DELIVER TO: TYLE DRY CLEANERS
RETURN TO: THE MENAGERIE HOTEL
GUEST NAME: ANNA CONDA, ROOM 401
DATE SENT: SATURDAY, OCTOBER 14
TIME SENT: 11:02 A.M.
PRIORITY: *Urgent! Return Laundry ASAP!*

Rhett,

I'm all for high drama, but really, "LAW Remember Me" is taking it a bit far. Surely you have ways (e.g., food and water) to control the artist better.

I say we go back to the earlier style. Either that or get rid of the stupid beast. This monkey business has gone on long enough.

And please don't say I'm being cold-blooded. This writing nonsense is simply too risky.

XX
Anna

51541

Tyle Dry Cleaners

Sp●ts, Stains and Wrinkles Removed with a Twinkle

Here are your clothes—cleaned to perfection!

PLEASE DELIVER TO:	**LAUNDRY RETURNED:**
ANNA CONDA ROOM 401, The Menagerie Hotel Tyle-O-Tropolis	12:01 P.M.

Relax, Anna.

This latest painting has the whole world buzzing! News crews have been out at the zoo all day and attendance is already over 3,500!

This could be the best marketing gimmick yet. You know how people love a good sideshow. We're just giving the fans what they want. Remember our Hong Kong tour?

EXCITEMENT! DRAMA! SURPRISE!
GIVE 'EM SOMETHING THAT'LL DAZZLE THEIR EYES!

I'm telling you, Skinny, the chump is smarter than we thought. This whole game is like a beautiful snake, constantly shedding its skin and turning in unexpected directions. We're right where we want to be on this. Trust me.

I'll stop by your lair soon for a visit.

Rhett

One-hour service guaranteed with a smile . . . or my name isn't Tyle!

THE MENAGERIE HOTEL

Tyleville, Missouri
A Tyle Entertainment Property

NAME: Lily A. Watson
GRADE: 6
TEACHER: Mr. Holmes
JOURNAL ENTRY FOR: Saturday, October 14, 7:30 p.m.

This has been the weirdest day. It's hard to explain. I don't feel sick or anything. But my mind keeps focusing on one thing and I can't stop thinking about it. Maybe writing it down will help me figure it out.

Today is Saturday and the courthouse is closed. Even though we have the day off from jury duty, we're still sequestered. So at 6 a.m., Fawn and I took our morning constitutional with Madame up and down the fourth floor hallway.

After that I took a shower, did my teeth exercises, got dressed (shorts today since we're not in court), and spent ten minutes walking on my hands. At 7:45, the whole jury met at the elevator and rode down to Rhett's Roost on the first floor. It's a really cool restaurant. You have to climb inside the tables, which are shaped like big nests.

(And don't even ask how Dr. L. E. Font got in. He lost his balance and went over rear end first. He landed on the eggs in the middle of the nest, which are really big cinnamon rolls. I swear that guy has cavities in his **brain**.)

Anyway, I ordered a Texas omelet, but I forgot to tell the waiter to hold the green peppers, so I had to pick them out one by one, which was completely dizzzgusting.

After breakfast, the bailiff took us to a private lounge on the third floor of the hotel. What a view! We got to watch the trapeze show for a while—from front row seats! When it was over, we had a couple of hours to just relax. The adults drank coffee. I had hot chocolate. Dr. L. E. Font and Sy Meese (the tuna guy) played Scrabble. Some of the others played bridge and Leon drew sketches.

Everyone else just sat around, reading the newspaper. Of course all the news about the trial was clipped out, but we could read parts of the paper, like the comics, the sports section, the classified ads, and a big front-page article about Priscilla.

OK, this is where it starts getting strange. You probably saw the latest painting by Priscilla. It says: "LAW Remember Me."

Well, maybe this sounds crazy, but my initials are L.A.W.: Lily Annabel Watson. I know this sounds nuts, but it almost seems like Perry is trying to talk to me . . . **from the grave.** Or maybe his spirit is in Priscilla, which is freaking me out just thinking about it.

The bad thing is I can't talk about this to anybody, not even Fawn, since it has to do with Perry and the trial. I guess I could talk to Madame about it, but then I'd know I really AM nuts.

Maybe I'm going crackers from being locked up in this hotel and I'm seeing things in paintings that aren't there. I told the counselor at school last year that I had so many thoughts swirling around in my head, I thought my brain was going to explode. She said that's normal and just part of growing up.

I can just see my brain exploding some day all over the gym floor and the counselor saying, "Now, Lily, couldn't you have put a towel down before you did that?"

I guess what I'll do is just sleep on it and see how I feel in the morning. Sometimes I get good ideas in my dreams.

By the way, I'll bet $20 you're not even reading this. But if I'm wrong, do not show this stupid journal to ANYONE! And don't you dare TELL anyone my middle name is Annabel.

I won't.

I mean it.

I know you do.

LILY WATSON'S JOURNAL
AND
last minute
RESEARCH PAPER

PART THREE
Things Start Getting Weird

The Tyleville Quill

Tyle Publishing
Rhett Tyle, Publisher

50 cents.......................................Monday, October 16......................Morning Edition

"Dear Priscilla":
Tyleville's first-class ape becomes nation's favorite addressee

Priscilla the gorilla is not only the world's most famous painter. Her mailbox has become the most popular destination for letters written in the United States. Officials with the U.S. Postal Service estimate that one out of every seven letters delivered today is addressed to Priscilla the gorilla.

"We've never seen anything like it before," Tyleville Postmaster Ken Guru said yesterday. "We've had to bring in dump trucks to deliver all of Priscilla's fan mail."

Since Priscilla began painting on the walls of her cage in August, more than five million letters addressed to "Priscilla the Gorilla, U.S.A." have been delivered to Tyle Park Zoo.

"That's more than the President of the United States and Santa Claus get combined," said Postmaster Guru.

Sociologists speculate that the letters to Priscilla reflect a national yearning for improved relations between humans and animals.

"Priscilla has tapped into our collective longing for a deeper connection to our friends in the animal world," explained Dr. Les Tawk. His colleague, Dr. Maura Huggs, agreed.

"It's not surprising that millions of people are writing to Priscilla," stated Dr. Huggs. "Priscilla is the people's primate. She represents the hopes and fears of a society alienated from the natural world. Plus, she's a good listener. Women in particular respond to Priscilla because, frankly, a lot of us don't feel validated in our human relationships with alpha males."

Tawk and Huggs will deliver a lecture next Tuesday entitled "Women Who Run with the Gorillas (and the Chumps Who Love Them)" at the Les Tawk–Maura Huggs Institute for Improved Interpersonal Relationships.

Priscilla poses with her 5 millionth letter

What's the Buzz

by
Bernie "Buzz" Ard

Another day, another column.

Anybody still reading an old geezer like me? Didn't think so.

Blame it on this last week of sequestration, but lately my life feels like a prison. With a daily deadline hanging over my head, I feel like that old boy Sisyphus.

Remember him? He's the mythical fella who had to push a huge boulder up a steep hill every day. Problem was, the darn rock rolled back down on him every night. So that's how he spent his days–rolling the stone up the hill, then being rolled over by it.

Boy, can I relate to that.

And I'm the guy who was going to write the Great American Novel? Ha. Turns out I was destined for smaller things, like this half-baked gossip column. Instead of wowing them with best-selling novels, I've become the Great American Hack Writer. GAHW, for short. Sounds like how I feel some days.

But I didn't mean to dump all this on you, Gentle Reader. Last thing I want to do is spoil anybody's cornflakes.

I did tell you, didn't I, that juror 12 is teaching me to walk on my hands? Who said you can't teach an old dog new tricks?

And it's official: juror 11 and I are no longer speaking. Her decision, not mine. She got miffed when I commented how dolled up she gets each day for jury duty. I mean, come on. Is this jury duty or a New York fashion show? Hard to tell by looking at this clotheshorse. Each morning she's dressed to kill. One day it's a reptile-print pantsuit with matching hat, shoes, and handbag. The next day it's a rattlesnake motif–dress, shoes, belt, purse–all with rattles. When I asked if she was venomous, she nearly bit my head off.

"Fashion," juror 11 told me, "is something you'll never understand, Mr. rumpled trousers and mustard-stained tie."

Yowch! The woman's so cold, she can give you frostbite. Oh, well. So I'm a fashion failure. *C'est le viski.*

Shabbily yours,

"Buzz"

CLASSIFIEDS

OCTOBUR 16

IM TEECHING THESE RATS TO EAT RITE OWT OF MY HANDS.
THERE REEL GOOD AT IT. I THINK THEY MUST REELY LOVE
THESE CHEESE SANDWIDGES.

I GOT ABOWT 7 OF THEM NOW WHO COME VIZIT ME AT NITE
AFTER DINNER. CHEESE SANDWIDGES STILL. I GIVE THEM HAVE
AND EAT THE OTHUR HAVE MYSELF. IT SEEMS PURTY FARE TO
ME CAWS IM ABOUT AS BIG AS 7 OF THEM PUT TOGATHUR.
THEY SEEM TO LIKE IT REEL WELL.

IM JEST GLAD THESE RATS ARENT OVUR AT THE ZOO. THEY
WOODNT SIRVIVE TEN MINITS OVUR THERE. NOT WITH THE WAY
MISTER TYLE DOZ THINGS. HE WOOD FEED THEM TO HIS SNAYKS
IN A SECUND.

BUT IM TRYIN NOT TO THINK ABOT MISTUR TYLE AND HIS
SNAYKS. IM JEST HOPIN HE DIDNT FEED PERRY TO THOSE
SNAYKS. AND ESPASHLY NOT TO THAT OLD KING KOBRA. HE
WOOD SWALLO PERRY IN 1 BITE.

I DON EVEN LIKE THINKIN ABOWT THET. IT MAKES ME TO
SAD. I DON LIKE THINKIN ABOWT THE TRYAL EETHER. THET
MAKES ME A LITTLE SCERED CAUSE I DON NO WHAT COOD
HAPPEN TO ME.

SO THETS WHY I JEST THINK ABOUT THESE RATS HERE AND
HOW MUCH THEY LOVE THESE CHEESE SANDWIDGES.

~~MY AUTOBIOGRAPHY~~
~~BY~~
~~FAWN PAPILLON~~

~~CHAPTER ONE~~
Tuesday evening

Never mind the silly autobiography. I'm starting to make sense of this melancholy I've been feeling. And all because of a Chinese fortune cookie I had for dessert tonight.

Here's what the fortune said:

Freedom is the greatest gift.

Exactly! No wonder Priscilla's blue. She's behind bars! So is that poor man on trial. And the birds in this hotel. And me–who just installed a new privacy fence and security system at my estate.

What a fool I've been, hiding for years behind these sunglasses and the walls of my estate. Aren't I the silly goose?

Tut tut! Yes, freedom is the greatest gift, as the cookie says. Now I must be a smart cookie and free myself–and these other poor caged creatures.

I wonder if Lily will help me. I must ask her.

∽ THE MENAGERIE HOTEL ∞

Tyleville, Missouri

A Tyle Entertainment Property

NAME: Lily A. Watson

GRADE: 6

TEACHER: Mr. Holmes

JOURNAL ENTRY FOR: Tuesday, October 17, 11:30 p.m.

I just woke up from the scariest dream.

All the jurors were cleaning cages in the zoo. Judge Gall and Mally Mute were there, too, but Mally looked like Fawn. (You know how everything's all turned around in dreams.) I was cleaning one cage after another and not really paying attention. Then I came to a cage with Bob White, who had become a werewolf with fangs and claws. Anna Conda started screaming, "Run for your life!" But then I heard Perry's voice from far away saying, "Lily, save me! Please!" I tried to run away so I wouldn't have to get in the cage with Bob White, but the judge told me I had to. Then I was flying in the sky and I started falling into a big dark pit and I tried to scream but no one could hear me and . . .

I HATE DREAMS LIKE THAT! I haven't had one that scary since the summer before fourth grade when I went to camp and heard the world's scariest ghost stories. I had to sleep with the light on for almost the whole summer, which was v. embarrassing, especially when I had friends spend the night. (Especially when we went back to school and Ashley told the whole class. Grrrr . . .)

I bet tonight's dream was somehow related to that story I read in the newspaper about Priscilla writing that weird message: "LAW Remember Me." There's no way "LAW" means me, right? RIGHT? And even if it did, what the heck am I supposed to do about it?

Oh my gosh. I just heard a creepy noise outside my window. Like someone crying. Or maybe it was a cat. Or a bird? The wind?

Ugh. The worst part of nightmares is trying to forget them and fall back asleep. I wish it would just hurry up and be morning. Maybe I'll paint something for Robin to take my mind off it.

THE MENAGERIE HOTEL
Guest Comment Card

Hi, Robin!

Here's another painting for you. Hope you like it.

Lily Watson

P.S. Sorry I have to keep writing these notes to you, but I never see you. I have to leave for jury duty at 7:15 a.m. and I don't get back till after 6:00 p.m.

P.P.S. Is there any chance I could get a night-light in my room? If not, no big deal.

October 18

Lily,

Another lovely painting. Thank you!

You'll find two night-lights, one installed on either side of your bed. I hope these meet with your satisfaction.

If you need anything else, please don't hesitate to ask.

Sincerely,

Robin

Housekeeping Department

P.S. We must just miss each other. I work from 8:00 a.m. to 5:00 p.m. I would stay later to say hello in person, but I have another job at night.

The Tyleville Quill

Tyle Publishing
Rhett Tyle, Publisher

50 cents......................Wednesday, October 18.................Afternoon Edition

Priscilla writes again:
"COME VISIT THE ZOO"

Zoo owner Rhett Tyle answers questions during a press conference

Well, she's done it again.

A new message in a painting was discovered yesterday in Priscilla the gorilla's cage.

"COME VISIT THE ZOO" were the words written in bold letters on a large canvas hanging in Priscilla's cage at Tyle Park Zoo.

Language experts from around the world were impressed by Priscilla's command of the English language and her sentence construction.

"These carefully chosen words tell us a lot about Priscilla," said Dick Shunary, professor of linguistics at Tyle University.

"It's obvious that Priscilla has a clear sense of herself and her environment,"

Shunary stated. "And the invitation to visit the zoo shows what a remarkably social creature she is."

Some skeptics, however, see Priscilla's latest painting as a crass marketing scheme by zoo officials to boost attendance. Zoo owner Rhett Tyle firmly denies the allegation.

"That really burns my toast when people talk that way," Tyle said at a press conference. "You think I'd tell Priscilla what to write? You think I'd write those words myself? Take a handwriting sample, if you don't believe me. Let's go *mano a mano!* Now then, anybody want to get their picture taken with Miss Priscilla? I'm giving a special discount today only. Step right up!"

Mother of murdered boy testifies in Bob White trial

Eleanor Keet, mother of Perry Keet, testified Monday in the murder trial of Bob White.

"Perry loved animals more than anything in the whole world," Eleanor Keet told the jury. "That's why he wanted to volunteer at the zoo. He wanted experience working with animals so he could become

a veterinarian."

But Perry Keet never made it to vet school. He never even made it to sixth grade. Last July 24, the 11-year-old boy

Eleanor Keet

(Continued on page 2, column 2)

What's the Buzz
by
Bernie "Buzz" Ard

One word: Heartbreaking.

How else could you describe Eleanor Keet's testimony?

Hard to imagine how people survive such unbearable sadness.

Not surprisingly, the jury had a quiet dinner Monday night. No one was in the mood for lighthearted conversation or jokes. Even the card players, a normally giggly bunch, were more somber than usual during their nightly bridge game. The rest of us followed suit.

Deal me out.

On a lighter note: juror 5 (a.k.a. Molar Boy) greeted us this morning at breakfast without his two front teeth. Seems the toothmeister slipped while getting out of the bathtub last night and broke off both teeth at the gum line.

Just goes to prove that the universe sometimes has a biting sense of humor.

Of course none of us knew what to say. Juror 9 started to let out a belly laugh but swallowed it in time, blaming it on a tough hash brown. (How lame is *that*?)

The rest of us did our best to turn our chortles into coughs and sneezes.

Finally, our youngest member (juror 12) put her arm around the toothless wonder's shoulder and said, "Don't worry. Corn-on-the-cob season is nine months away."

Even old Molar Boy had to smile at that.

With his mouth closed.

"Buzz"

(From page 1)

disappeared from the zoo.

"He said he'd be home in time for supper at six o'clock," Eleanor Keet told the packed courtroom in the Tyle County Courthouse. "My husband and I waited and waited. Finally at seven-thirty, we called the police."

On cross-examination, defense attorney Mallory Mute asked Eleanor Keet if she had any reason to believe her son was afraid of Bob White or disliked working with him.

"Perry liked everyone," Mrs. Keet replied, stopping to wipe her tears with a handkerchief. "He never had a bad word to say about anyone. And look where it got him."

Police Chief Jay Byrd is expected to testify on Friday.

CLASSIFIEDS

Sewing & alterations. Costumes are my specialty. Robin: 555-5760

Got rats? Call us. Reasonable rates. 555-TYLE

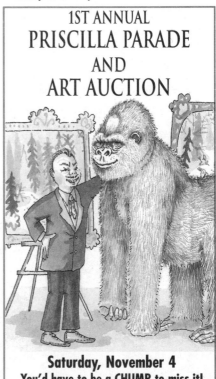

1ST ANNUAL
PRISCILLA PARADE
AND
ART AUCTION

Saturday, November 4
You'd have to be a CHUMP to miss it!

NAME: Lily A. Watson

GRADE: 6

TEACHER: Mr. Holmes

JOURNAL ENTRY FOR: Wednesday, October 18, 8:30 p.m.

I don't care if you think I'm crazy. The new painting by Priscilla is a DIRECT ANSWER to the question I wrote in my journal last night.

Remember when I was trying to convince myself that Priscilla's painting was NOT a secret message to me? Because even if it was, what the heck could I do about it?

Well, now we've got this latest painting with the message: "Come Visit The Zoo."

Don't you think that's a **little odd**? Or is it me who's odd? Maybe it's just that I haven't been able to watch TV since I got here, and my mind is making this stuff up—like it's a movie of the week or something.

But what if it's not made up? What if Perry really IS talking to me from the grave? Or—and this is even creepier—maybe he's channeling through Priscilla. I feel like I should do something or tell someone. But if I do, I could get kicked off the jury for weirdness. (Can they do that?)

This is the kind of stuff I get in trouble for at school. The teachers say I'm always looking for trouble where there's none. But this is different! I've got to figure out what to do. And I've

GOT to figure out how this stupid air conditioner works. It's been so hot all week, so I turned the a/c on HIGH again last night. When I woke up, there was frost on the *inside* of my window. Maybe that's my problem. Maybe my brain froze and shrunk. Or do things expand when they get cold?

See what I mean? I'm forgetting **EVERYTHING** I know about **EVERYTHING!** I'm turning off this dang air conditioner right this minute and opening the windows. Cripes, maybe my dad was right about not letting me touch the air conditioner at home.

I wish I could ask him and my mom what to do about all this. I haven't seen or talked to them in 13 days. That's as long as summer camp and I never get homesick at camp. But this feels different. I had to bite my hand twice today to keep from crying for no reason. It's hard to explain. I hope you don't think I'm a big fathead because I keep rambling on about what's going on in my brain. But that's the assignment, right? If I've been doing this whole blah blah blah journal wrong, I'm going to drop out of school for sure.

DELIVER TO: TYLE DRY CLEANERS
RETURN TO: THE MENAGERIE HOTEL
GUEST NAME: ANNA CONDA, ROOM 401
DATE SENT: THURSDAY, OCTOBER 19
TIME SENT: 6:33 P.M.
PRIORITY: *Regular*

Rhett,

Saw the photo of Priscilla's new painting in the paper yesterday morning. Brilliant! Toss an extra banana to the monkey.

XXOO Anna

P.S. My creative juices have been overflowing, too! I'm thinking of adding a furniture line to the House of S-Tyle collection.

House of S-Tyle Presents . . .

Furniture to Die For

Please increase the feeding program. I'll need oodles of large skins for this collection.

53541

Tyle Dry Cleaners

Sp●ts, Stains and Wrinkles Removed with a Twinkle

Here are your clothes—cleaned to perfection!

PLEASE DELIVER TO:	LAUNDRY RETURNED:
ANNA CONDA ROOM 401, The Menagerie Hotel Tyle-O-Tropolis	⌐7:32 P.M.⌐

Anna,

The new designs are sssssssensational. I'll throw an extra dozen rats in the pit to fatten the fellas up.

Gotta cut this short. I want to get down to the police station and talk to Jay Byrd before he testifies tomorrow.

XO

Rhett

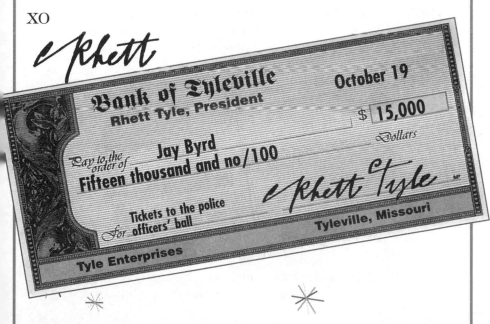

Bank of Tyleville
Rhett Tyle, President

October 19

$ 15,000

Pay to the order of   Jay Byrd

Fifteen thousand and no/100   *Dollars*

Rhett Tyle

For   Tickets to the police officers' ball

Tyleville, Missouri

Tyle Enterprises

One-hour service guaranteed with a smile . . . or my name isn't Tyle!

K-TYLE FM 100
TyleRadio for Tyleville
Transcript
Friday, October 20

KEN AIRY: Live from the majestic studios of K-TYLE atop Tyle-O-Tropolis in downtown Tyleville, this is Ken Airy with K-TYLE news on the hour. The Bob White trial tops the news. Reporter Maggie Pie is standing by with details of the day's events. Maggie, what can you tell us?

MAGGIE PIE: Well, Ken, the prosecution really started getting tough today in building its case against Bob White. Prosecutor Golden Ray Treevor called Police Chief Jay Byrd to the stand. Treevor asked Byrd to tell the court the nickname police officers had for Bob White.

KEN AIRY: Nickname?

MAGGIE PIE: Yes, it seems many members of the Tyleville police force referred to White as the "Tyle County kook" because of his bizarre behavior. Police Chief Byrd testified that White had a routine of riding his bike along Highway 60 every morning. If he came upon an animal that had been killed -- a dog or cat or even a rat -- White would stop, pull the dead animal off the highway, and bury it by the side of the road. Byrd said Bob White often rode 40 miles a day, performing this strange ritual.

KEN AIRY: Burying dead animals on the side of the highway? I think we can safely call that odd.

MAGGIE PIE: Odd, yes. But not illegal, which was the point defense attorney Mally Mute made in her cross-examination. Mute asked Police Chief Byrd if any of Bob White's odd habits were illegal. Byrd hesitated a bit before finally responding no. Mute also attempted to discredit Byrd and the entire Tyleville police force for closing the Keet investigation when White confessed to the murder, just hours after Perry Keet's disappearance.

KEN AIRY: Very interesting, Maggie. How did the jurors respond to Byrd's testimony?

MAGGIE PIE: They were hard to read, Ken. And remember, we won't know what the jurors are thinking until they deliver their verdict at the end of the trial.

KEN AIRY: What are you hearing outside the courtroom?

MAGGIE PIE: Let's ask. Excuse me, sir. What do you think about Bob White and his bizarre animal-burying rituals?

UNIDENTIFIED MAN: The man is an animal himself. I wouldn't trust him with my dog.

MAGGIE PIE: Ma'am, how about you? Does it bother you that Police Chief Jay Byrd called off the Keet investigation as soon as Bob White confessed?

UNIDENTIFIED WOMAN: Well, I suppose the police could've spent more time trying to find the little boy's body. But what good would that have done Mr. and Mrs. Keet? Their son was murdered. Why waste taxpayers' money keeping an investigation open when Bob White said he did it? Case closed.

MAGGIE PIE: Back to you, Ken.

MY AUTOBIOGRAPHY
BY
FAWN PAPILLON

CHAPTER ONE
Friday, quite late

So the prosecution is painting Bob White as a kook, all because his only friends are animals. Of all things!

From the beginning, Bob White has reminded me of a stray animal. Not pathetic. And certainly not dangerous. Just a weak man who was bullied by the system, like so many of us who end up in cages.

Speaking of cages, after dinner tonight I fed several of the birds in the hotel lobby with a dinner roll I saved from Rhettalini's. I even petted a macaw through the bars of his cage. Such a beautiful creature! Why anyone would want to put a bird in a cage is beyond me. I wonder if they're ever allowed to fly free or if they're always under lock and key. I suspect the latter. A shameful pity.

Lily saw me tearing off bits of the dinner roll. She suggested we let the birds out some night. "Just for fun," as she put it. Ah, a girl after my own troublemaking heart!

That reminds me: I'm looking forward to a little trouble myself. Tonight!

Details to followwwwwwwwww. Fplshtast! I'll never get used to this cursed compl%u ter.

"Birds of a Feather"
Lobby, Menagerie Hotel
10·20
Leon D. Vinci

THE MENAGERIE HOTEL

Tyleville, Missouri
A Tyle Entertainment Property

NAME: Lily A. Watson
GRADE: 6
TEACHER: Mr. Holmes
JOURNAL ENTRY FOR: Friday, October 20, 10:30 p.m.

After dinner tonight (I had ravioli and blueberry cheesecake), Fawn taught me how to play solitaire with two decks of cards. It's her favorite game. Once she played solitaire for three days straight without sleeping, which is the most depressing thing I've ever heard.

I mean, here she is, this famous movie star, and she sits at home playing solitaire? I'm about .00000000000000000001 as popular as she is, and even I don't do that. (And if I did, I would never in a million years admit it.)

There have been plenty of times when I wasn't invited to sleepovers and birthday parties, especially in fourth grade, which we're not even going to discuss here. But even when I was the **ONLY ONE** who wasn't invited to the back-to-school sleepover, I never told my friends (or so-called friends) that I stayed home with my mom and dad and worked on that stupid 10,000-piece puzzle of Mount Rushmore, which it turns out had only 9,997 pieces.

I stayed up till 11:30 that night writing the puzzle manufacturer a letter. The next summer they sent me a button that says "I Go to Pieces Over Puzzles!" Sometimes I think people are *trying* to drive me crazy. Now that I think about it, though, it was nice of my mom and dad to do that puzzle with me. I wonder if they were just trying to make me feel better for not being popular.

At least I'm not as unpopular as Bob White. We found out today in court that the police call him the "Tyle County kook." Cripes. It's just like at school when the boys call me dumb names like Lily Pad (as if that's even funny) and Frilly Lilly because once I wore a fancy-dancy blouse with ruffles for picture day.

I thought all these stupid nicknames would stop once I got out of school, but I guess people always say mean things about other people. It never stops, especially for people like Bob White. They get it the worst. But anybody who's even the least bit different gets it bad.

Remember when I said I was in the third-most popular group at school? Really, I'm not in a group at all. Well, sometimes I am. I usually bounce between the second-most popular and the third-most popular lunch table groups. But sometimes I just eat lunch by myself because I don't feel like dealing with the whole popularity game.

After dinner tonight I asked Fawn what it was like when she was the most popular movie star in the world. She said it was the loneliest time of her life, which makes ZERO sense to me. If I were popular, I would NEVER be lonely. Sometimes I think Fawn talks in riddles, but I still like her.

She said the problem with being a star was that people would see her in movies and feel like they knew her, even though they didn't. She said no one ever really knew her. I told her it's the same with being a kid. Every adult was once a kid so they all think they know eggggggsactly what you're going through, even though they're completely clueless.

As soon as I said that last part, I wanted to rip out my tongue because Fawn is one adult who's NOT clueless. But she didn't seem to mind at all. She made her funny crabby face and said, "Don't people drive you simply batty?" And then she pulled a dinner roll from her pocket and we fed the birds in the lobby.

Fawn said back when she was a star, the more film offers she turned down, the more popular she became. It's weird, but it made me think of Perry. He was never more popular than at his funeral. I guess people always want what they can't have.

I've got to stop thinking about my stupid popularity problems and start focusing on the trial again. But I can't stop thinking about that newspaper picture of Priscilla and her painting. It's giving me the chills just thinking about it. Do you think it's possible "Come Visit The Zoo" is an invitation to go see Priscilla? And if so, how in the world am I supposed to visit the zoo when I'm stuck here on jury duty?

Stuck here with a stomachache, I should say. I had three pieces of blueberry cheesecake tonight for dessert. (Buzz and Fawn both gave me theirs.) I feel like I'm getting bigger and bluer by the minute, like Violet Beauregarde in *Willy Wonka and the Chocolate Factory.*

Usually I love cheesecake. We always get cheesecake delivered from Pie-Thon Bakery when we're working on the school newspaper. Ordering cheesecake is the best part about being on the newspaper staff.

The second best part of working on the paper is doing devious things, like writing headlines where the first letter of every word spells out something. Last year, I wrote a story and gave it this headline: **7th Graders Survey Trends In New Knapsacks.** (Really, that's: 7th Graders STINK.) You can also slip in messages through fake ads in the classifieds, like: *Tandem bike 4 sale, call Eliza or Henry.* I put that one in last year when Eliza and Henry broke up. The teachers haven't caught on (and please don't tell), but all the kids do it. I started writing the fake ads last year after I read an old fogy mystery where the detectives sent sneaky messages to people through the classified ads.

I've got to sign off now so I can do my teeth exercises for an hour tonight. Dr. L. E. Font asked me again (for the **4,000,000th** time) when I'm getting braces. He said, "You don't want people calling you bucky beaver, do you?" I said, "Well, to tell you the truth, Dr. Font, I do. I mean, who wants boring old people teeth when, if you're lucky like me, you can have teeth like a beaver? I'm doing everything I can think of to keep them from straightening out. That whole perfectly straight teeth thing is so boring." He said, "Really? How very interesting. I must ponder that."

Argh! Forget it. I'm going to bed now and let my brain (and stomach) rest. I always think clearer in the morning anyway.

THE MENAGERIE HOTEL

Tyleville, Missouri
A Tyle Entertainment Property

October 21

The Honorable Judge E. Gall
Tyle County Courthouse
Tyleville, Missouri

Dear Judge,

I hope it's okay that I'm writing to you. I have a question and I wasn't sure how to ask it. At my school, we usually raise our hands when we have a question. But I don't think I can do that in the courtroom, so that's why I'm writing you this letter.

What I wanted to ask is this: Is there any chance the jurors could visit Tyle Park Zoo?

For one thing, I think it would help us understand the case better if we could see where Perry Keet and Bob White worked. It might give us a better idea of the crime scene.

Plus, I know everyone on the jury would LOVE to see Priscilla the gorilla. Since we can't discuss the trial, Priscilla's just about all we ever talk about at dinner and during court recesses. (I haven't had morning recess since third grade!)

Anyway, it's just an idea. Hope you'll think about it. I also hope you and your family are enjoying the nice autumn weather.

Sincerely,

Lily Watson

Juror 12

P.S. Cool robe! I have one at home sort of like it. I wore it last year for Halloween. (I went as Count Dracula.)

OCTOBUR 21

AT THE CORTHOUSE YESTURDAY THEY SED I WAS A WEERDO AND A KOOK. MEYBE I SHOOD TELL WHY I BERY THEM DED ANIMULS. MEYBE I SHOOD TELL WHAT MISTUR TYLE DOZ WHEN HE FINDS DED ANIMULS BY THE SIDE OF THE RODE.

BUT IF I TELL PEEPUL MISTUR TYLE WOULD KILL ME FOR SHURE AND FEED ME TO THE SNAYKS JEST LIKE HE PROBLY DID WITH PERRY.

THE GARD HEAR TOLD ME THE JURY MITE BE GOIN TOO THE ZOO. I WISH I COOD GO TO. I COOD GIV A REAL GOOD TOOR OF THE ZOO. I NO EVURY CADGE AND EVURY ANIMUL. I EVEN NO WATS GOING ON IN THE REPTYLE HOUSE. WEAR NOBODYS SOPOSED TO GO.

I SHOWD THAT WONCE TO PERRY CAWS HE KEPT AXING AND AXING TO SEE THE REPTYLE HOUSE. IT SCAIRED HIM BAD. I TOLD HIM I WAS SORRY FOR SCAIRING HIM AND HE SED IT WAS OK. I RECKON HE LIKED ANIMULS ALMOST AS MUTCH AS ME. HE DINDT LIKE TO SEE WHAT MISTUR TYLE WAS DOIN. I DINDNT EITHER. POOR PERRY. I HOPE IT WASENT THAT FAT OLD KING KOBRA THAT ATE HIM.

IM STARTIN TO GET MITEY TIRED OF CHEESE SANDWIDGES BUT THE RATS THEY STILL LIKES THEM SO IM NOT COMPLAYNING. THESE HEAR ARE GOOD RATS. THEIR LUCKY TO CAWS I WONT NEVER LET THEM BECOM SNAYK FOD.

I HOPE I LEFT ENUFF FOD OUT FOR MY DOGS.

The Tyleville Quill

Tyle Publishing
Rhett Tyle, Publisher

$1.50.............................Sunday, October 22...................Morning Edition

Bob White jury to visit Tyle Park Zoo

Jurors will get private tour of zoo on Thursday

Taking a break from courtroom duties, the jury in the Bob White trial will take a field trip to Tyle Park Zoo on Thursday. The 12-member jury plus two alternate jurors will be accompanied by police officers and attorneys on both sides of the Bob White case.

"This is an important opportunity for the jury to relive Perry Keet's final hours," prosecuting attorney Golden Ray Treevor told reporters. "I expect it will be an emotional experience for all of us."

For security purposes, the zoo will be closed to visitors during the jurors' one-hour visit. Protestors, including members of the Protect Our Children from What They Shouldn't Hear or See Organization, will not be allowed to march within 100 yards of the zoo entrance.

According to attorneys, jurors will be allowed to tour any part of the zoo they wish.

"It's important that the jurors have full access to the zoo," defense attorney Mally Mute explained.

Mute told reporters that the idea for the excursion to the zoo originated from the jury.

"The judge had a request from one of the jurors," Mute said. "After taking into account various security considerations, we all agreed it would be a good idea to let the jurors visit the zoo."

Legal strategists predict the prosecution will use the zoo visit to try to build sympathy for the victim, while the defense will emphasize the lack of clear and convincing evidence at the crime scene.

If nothing else, jurors will get a chance to see Priscilla the gorilla and her world-famous artwork before the paintings are auctioned off next month.

Handwriting analysis confirms Priscilla speaks for herself

Results are in from the handwriting analysis taken last week at Tyle Park Zoo. At a press conference yesterday, Rhett Tyle released the results and addressed skeptics

who suspected he was behind Priscilla's messages.

"You can kiss that crackpot theory

(Continued on page 2, column 2)

What's the Buzz

by

Bernie "Buzz" Ard

From the "Maybe it's just me, but . . ." department.

Since when is it weird to enjoy spending time alone? Since when is compassion for animals "kooky"?

I refer, of course, to the recent testimony by Police Chief Jay Byrd, who told tale after tale of Bob White's alleged "kookiness."

Waitaminnit. Begging everyone's pardon, but does the name Henry David Thoreau mean anything to anyone? How about Albert Einstein, a notorious recluse and, oh yeah, a genius? Does Emily Dickinson ring a bell for thee? She was only the pinup gal for the I-want-to-be-alone club. That reminds me of my favorite joke of last year: What did the grass seed from Transylvania say? I vant to be a lawn.

But seriously, folks, I've never spent more time alone than these last three weeks on jury duty. And I gotta tell you, it's not as easy as you think. You've got to be pretty comfortable in your own skin to be a loner. Being a social animal is much easier. You can lose yourself in the crowd and hide behind cornball jokes.

But being alone in a hotel room, night after night . . . well, it's just me and me, kid. And to tell you the truth, I'm a little underwhelmed by my own company.

If I had to guess, I'd say the real kooks are those of us who can't stand flying solo for more than five minutes. What does that say about us? (Don't answer that.)

If Bob White is a kook, well, let's shake, pal.

Other sequestration snippets: Our residentist (juror 5) made two temporary teeth out of wood putty to replace the choppers he broke last week. The toothmeister says he's "experidenting."

Better rest my own choppers and practice walking on my hands.

"Buzz"

Moo Goo Gi Tyle

A versa-Tyle
menu of
Chinese favorites,
including
Emperor Rhett's Ophidian Delight

This week's special:

Viper Lo Mein

(From page 1)

good-bye," said Tyle, who hired world-renowned handwriting expert Dr. Penny Menshep to study the words contained in Priscilla's paintings.

After careful scrutiny of Priscilla's handwriting, Dr. Menshep made the following statement: "It's clear to me that this is the handwriting of a friendly primate with a playful, harmless nature and a high I.Q. Needless to say, it is not the handwriting of Mr. Tyle."

DELIVER TO: TYLE DRY CLEANERS
RETURN TO: THE MENAGERIE HOTEL
GUEST NAME: ANNA CONDA, ROOM 401
DATE SENT: SUNDAY, OCTOBER 22
TIME SENT: 6 P.M.
PRIORITY: *ASAP!! URGENT!!*

Rhett,

Have you heard? We're visiting the ZOO!

There's no telling where the tour will lead. Rumor has it we'll be permitted to roam freely everywhere in the zoo for a whole hour. You've got to do something—quick! We'll be there Thursday.

I told you we should get rid of that stupid beast. I should've insisssssssssssssssssssssted.

Anna

55213

Tyle Dry Cleaners

Sp●ts, Stains and Wrinkles Removed with a Twinkle

Here are your clothes—cleaned to perfection!

PLEASE DELIVER TO:	LAUNDRY RETURNED:
ANNA CONDA ROOM 401, The Menagerie Hotel Tyle-O-Tropolis	⌐6:59 P.M.⌐

Calm down, my pet.

Have you forgotten? Disappearing acts are my specialty! Remember the show in Vienna, 1990?

TO HIDE A PRICELESS PIECE OF JEWELRY, OR ANYTHING FROM A TO Z, YOU MUST PRACTICE SIMPLICITY IN PLACING IT WHERE NO ONE WILL SEE:

(RIGHT IN FRONT OF THEIR EYES)

Never worry when you're in the hands of the Great Tylini, Master of Illusion! The plan is already in motion. Meet me tomorrow night at 10:30 on the fire escape outside your window. I'll tell you the details then.

Rhett

One-hour service guaranteed with a smile . . . or my name isn't Tyle!

SUMMONS
TO THE EXECUTIVE PENTHOUSE SUITE
of
RHETT TYLE

DATE: _Monday_   TIME: _8 A.M._

EMPLOYEE NAME: Robin

DEPARTMENT: Housekeeping

REASON FOR VISIT: Important business

PRIORITY: URGENT! Drop everything and get up here!

R. Tyle

ROBIN'S SEWING AND ALTERATIONS
Costumes Are My Specialty!

CUSTOMER ORDER FORM

CUSTOMER: Rhett Tyle

DATE ORDERED: Oct. 23

BILL TO: Rhett Tyle

DATE NEEDED: Oct. 26, morning

ITEM: Halloween costume

SIZE: small

FABRIC: fake fur (black)

NOTES:

Make it exactly like
Mr. Tyle said.

RUSH JOB!

URGENT

PRICE: $75.00

MY AUTOBIOGRAPHY
BY
FAWN PAPILLON

CHAPTER ONE

Monday, v. late

It's almost midnight and I'm just back from my fourth night of skinny-dipping in the hotel swimming pool. Absolutely invigorating!

I had forgotten how much I enjoy swimming without clothes. It makes one feel like a dolphin frolicking in the open sea. Perfectly marvelous!

No one has detected my nighttime adventures. The bailiff, bless his soul, nods off promptly at 10 p.m. That's when I tiptoe out of my room, cloaked only in darkness–and a bath towel. Fortunately the staircase is just outside my door. I descend the stairs to the second floor, where the swan-shaped pool awaits me.

I'm tempted to tell my dear friend Lily how I've been spending my evenings. But I'd hate to get the sweet thing in trouble, if trouble is indeed what awaits me. I must act innocent. Ha! Imagine, me–acting! First time in 50 years. Now this is fun.

Freedom IS the greatest gift! I intend to savor it like a French pastry.

Madame Butterfly is having a taste of freedom tonight, too. She's staying across the hall with Lily. No doubt they're both sound asleep like the innocent little lambs they are. Not a care in the world.

Ah, youth . . .

THE MENAGERIE HOTEL

Tyleville, Missouri

A Tyle Entertainment Property

NAME: Lily A. Watson

GRADE: 6

TEACHER: Mr. Holmes

JOURNAL ENTRY FOR: Tuesday, October 24, 3 a.m.

I've got a riddle for you.

Q: Why do they take the TVs out of jurors' hotel rooms?

A: Because **real** life is better than anything on TV!

With all the crazy things going on around here, I feel like I'm an actress on a TV detective show.

Here's what happened: It started off simple enough, just like on TV. I've been dropping hints to Fawn for a week that I'd like to have a sleepover with Madame in my room some night. During dinner at Nile Style Tyle, Fawn said I could.

So at 9 p.m., Fawn brought Madame to my door. It took Madame a little while to get used to the zebra stripes in my room, but after that she was fine. I had her doing all kinds of tricks, like jumping three feet in the air for a dog biscuit. I tried to teach her to stand on just her front paws (like a handsland) but no luck.

At around 10 p.m., I decided to give Madame a bath. Fawn gave me a special dog shampoo to use on Madame. It smells all pepperminty and makes her hair really silky. So I put Madame in the bathtub and lathered her up till she looked like a little lamb.

Before I rinsed the shampoo out, I took Madame out of the tub and sat her in the sink in front of the mirror and made funny hairdos on her. I squished the suds around to make little horns on her head. Then I made one big horn coming out of her head, like a unicorn.

It was cracking me up. I think Madame liked it, too. I wanted to paint a picture of her all sudsy like that to give to Fawn. So I told Madame to sit still while I got my paints, the ones Leon gave me, which were in my closet.

BIG GIANT HUGE MISTAKE! No sooner had I turned my back to get my watercolors than Madame was gone! Off the sink. Out of the bathroom. Over my bed. And out the window!

I told you I'd turned off the air conditioner in here and opened the windows, right? (Another **BIG MISTAKE.**) Well, before I could even set my paints down, Madame was out on the fire escape, just sitting there, all sudsy, with her tongue wagging and smiling that crazy dog smile.

But here's where it really starts getting like a TV show: Guess who else was out on the fire escape. Anna Conda and Rhett Tyle! And guess what they were doing. Kissing!! Between kisses, Anna kept saying, "You're brilliant! You're brilliant!" to Mr. Tyle.

Aha!

I thought I was going to have a stroke. I stepped away from the window real quick so they wouldn't see me. I'm pretty sure they didn't. But, cripes, I didn't know what to do. Should I go get Fawn? Send for the bailiff? Call the judge?

My brain was practically ERUPTING with all these questions. I just sat down on my bed and put my head in my hands, which were still soapy with dog shampoo. I think I even started crying a little bit. It's just that I was so nervous about what might happen to Madame. There she was, sitting on this little tiny edge of the fire escape, and there was no way I could reach her. What if she fell four floors down and died? How would I ever break the news to Fawn?

Well, wouldn't you know just then I felt a big, wet THWUMP on my lap. And there was Madame, panting away.

I closed the window and carried Madame back to the bathroom. I rinsed her off in the tub and dried her with a towel. Then I brushed her hair for a little while, which she loved. I turned off the light and put her in bed. I crawled in next to her. She smelled all minty and nice. I think she fell asleep in about two seconds flat.

But my mind was racing. What would I have done if she'd fallen off the fire escape and died? And what in heck were Anna Conda and Rhett Tyle doing on the fire escape? I mean, I KNOW what they were doing, but what did it mean? I was thinking and thinking and thinking . . . and then I must've fallen asleep.

Now it's after 3 o'clock in the morning and I'm wide awake. I can't stop thinking about Anna Conda and Rhett Tyle. He's supposed to testify in court in a couple of days. That can't be fair for them to be kissing like that when he's the star witness for the prosecution and she's on the jury, can it? I don't think so. But who can I tell? That's the real riddle.

The answer, I guess, is my journal. I better get a good grade on this thing because I'm telling you EVERYTHING—even about people KISSING.

I still have so much to think about, like if I'm dreaming all this about Perry. Maybe it was just my imagination. But what if it's real? What if Perry has become an invisible spirit? What if he

135

really is sending me messages from the grave?

I've got to come up with a strategy. And there's no time to waste since our field trip to the zoo is the day after tomorrow. That was my idea, but now I'm afraid it might be completely creepy to stand in the same spot where Bob White killed Perry. I can't even think about it or I'll have nightmares.

Right now I'm too tired to do anything but sleep. No teeth exercises tonight. And if I start getting Timbuktooth because of all this, I'm going to scream.

I have to get up for my constitutional with Fawn and Madame in less than three hours. Maybe then I'll feel smarter.

4 a.m. Agh! Still can't sleep. Might as well paint.

5:45 a.m. Still awake. Zero sleep all night. I feel like a slumber party zombie. But at least I thought of a plan.

THE MENAGERIE HOTEL
Guest Comment Card

October 24

Good morning, Robin! (Or good afternoon, if you're reading this after 12:00.)

Were you serious when you wrote that I should feel free to ask you if I needed anything? Because I do. I need to put a classified ad in *The Tyleville Quill*.

I'm not sure how much it costs, but here's $5. If it's not enough, let me know and I'll leave more money tomorrow.

I keep meaning to ask you if you make your bed at home every day. If I had your job, I'd never make my own bed. But I bet your house is probably spotless, with all the beds made and the whole house vacuumed every day, right? My dad says I'm like nature because I abhor a vacuum.

Anyway, thanks for answering all my questions and buying the ad for me.

Your friend on the fourth floor,

Lily Watson

P.S. Maybe after the trial, we can meet for lunch or something. Do you like shrimp cocktail?

My classified ad for
The Tyleville Quill

10/24

Dear Lily,

Thanks for your note. Your room has become my favorite stop on the fourth floor. I'll try to answer your questions in order.

I'd be happy to place the ad for you. I buy classified ads several times every week for my sewing business. I'll buy one for you when I purchase mine. The ads cost $5, so we're even. Your ad will appear in tomorrow's paper.

I make my bed at home every day. It's just a habit. But the rest of my house isn't as spotless as you might think. Right now I'm in the middle of sewing a Halloween costume, and my living room is covered with scraps of material.

I would love to get together for lunch after the trial ends.

Until then,

Robin

Oops. Missed one.

No, I've never had shrimp cocktail. I don't drink alcohol.

The Tyleville Quill

Tyle Publishing
Rhett Tyle, Publisher

50 cents.......................Wednesday, October 25...............Afternoon Edition

Buyers from around the world coming for art auction

Rhett Tyle prepares for upcoming art auction

Art buyers from Peoria to Pretoria are scheduled to arrive in Tyleville a week from Saturday to bid on original gorilla artwork at the First Annual Priscilla Art Auction.

"Everybody who's anybody is coming for the auction," said Rhett Tyle, organizer of the event. "I've had calls from buyers in Bombay who want to get their hands on a Priscilla original."

According to Tyle, Priscilla's recent paintings will bring more than $1 million each.

"And that's a bargain!" said Tyle. "Where else are you going to find bona fide gorilla artwork?"

The First Annual Priscilla Art Auction will be held in the Rhett-unda of the Grand Lobby in The Menagerie Hotel immediately following the Priscilla Parade.

What's the Buzz

by

Bernie "Buzz" Ard

Know what I love about jury duty? The furniture.

Call me a sucker for pomp and circumstance, but I love that big old raised desk the judge sits behind. Folks in the know call it the judge's *bench.*

And notice how you can only see the judge from the shoulders up. I hear it's a holdover from the old days, when judges needed the protection. How clever is that? I mean, think about it: The judge's bench is like a big, wooden bulletproof jacket. Guess things were pretty rough back in the early days of law 'n order.

The rest of the courtroom is pretty much what you've seen on TV. The witnesses sit in a smallish chair next to and below the judge. Both the judge and the witness face the attorneys and the defendant, who sit at long wooden tables. The jurors sit on the side, so we can see all the action.

It's a serious scene. But I can't help wondering: Who has to polish all the wood furniture in this place?

"Buzz"

K-TYLE FM 100
TyleRadio for Tyleville
Transcript
Thursday, October 26

KEN AIRY: Live from the majestic studios of K-TYLE atop Tyle-O-Tropolis in downtown Tyleville, this is Ken Airy with K-TYLE news on the hour. Jurors in the Bob White trial got a big surprise today when they toured Tyle Park Zoo. K-TYLE TV's Maggie Pie is covering the story. Maggie, I hear you have quite a story for us.

MAGGIE PIE: That's right, Ken. What a day! As you know, jurors in the Bob White trial were expecting a well-deserved break today when they visited the zoo. But they got more than that. I'm wearing my Tyle-Cam headpiece and zooming in on Priscilla's cage in the distance. Viewers tuned to K-TYLE TV can get a look at what jurors saw this morning when they arrived at the zoo. Can you see him, Ken? The cage has been moved back about 50 yards.

KEN AIRY: Give me a second to adjust my monitor. Okay. There. What the -- ? Is that another gorilla in the cage with Priscilla?

MAGGIE PIE: Sure is. Isn't he adorable? And can you see the sign he's holding?

KEN AIRY: Yes, I can. I'm trying to make out the words.

MAGGIE PIE: The sign says, "HELP ME LAW!" An amazing thing for a young gorilla to write, don't you think? I have zoo owner Rhett Tyle standing by to tell us all about this recent arrival to Tyle Park Zoo. Mr. Tyle, who is the little fellow?

RHETT TYLE: That there is Priscilla's nephew.

MAGGIE PIE: Where'd he come from?

RHETT TYLE: Uh, (cough) well, it's a little complicated. See, Priscilla here has a sister named Penelope who lives in Pittsburgh, Pennsylvania. And she -- Penelope, I mean -- had this little gorilla baby a couple of years ago. Well now, Penelope couldn't keep the baby. Trouble in the family, if you know what I mean. So anyhoo, the people at her zoo asked if we could care for the kid gorilla.

MAGGIE PIE: I see. And what's his name?

RHETT TYLE: His name? Why, it's uh . . . er . . . Larry.

MAGGIE PIE: Larry?

RHETT TYLE: That's right. Larry. Larry, the kid gorilla.

MAGGIE PIE: He's a cutie, all right. But why has the cage been moved back so far? I can barely make out the gorillas' faces.

RHETT TYLE: Well, see, Larry's a shy duck. Doesn't like people too much. Needs his personal space. He's a little cold-blooded. Kind of like some women I know.

MAGGIE PIE: I beg your pardon.

RHETT TYLE: Not you, Maggie!

MAGGIE PIE: Oh. Well, it looks like his aunt Priscilla has already taught Larry how to write. How do you interpret the sign Larry's holding?

RHETT TYLE: Well, I don't see that it needs much interpretation. Larry must've known the

141

jurors were coming to visit, so he painted them a friendly sign. "HELP ME LAW!" is Larry's way of saying "Help me, you law-abiding citizens on the jury, convict the murderous thug named Bob White who, with his bare hands and dirty fingernails, killed an innocent little boy, thereby preventing him from attending the First Annual Priscilla Parade and Art Auction on November 4th in beautiful downtown Tyleville."

MAGGIE PIE: Truly amazing. Thank you, Mr. Tyle. Back to you, Ken.

THE MENAGERIE HOTEL

Tyleville, Missouri
A Tyle Entertainment Property

NAME: Lily A. Watson

GRADE: 6

TEACHER: Mr. Holmes

JOURNAL ENTRY FOR: Thursday, October 26, 8:00 p.m.

WRITE ON!

Aunt Priscilla meets long-lost nephew; teaches little guy to write

Jurors in the Bob White trial got a special welcome today from Larry the gorilla, a recent arrival to Tyle Park Zoo. According to zoo owner Rhett Tyle, Larry is the nephew of Priscilla, the amazing gorilla who apparently has been sharing her linguistic talents with her new roommate at the zoo.

He's So Shy;

Zoo owner explains Larry's need for privacy

Tyle announces plans to create a natural gorilla habitat at zoo.

Look at this newspaper article. See the sign the little gorilla is holding? It says "HELP ME LAW!"

Everyone on the jury says it meant all of us, since we're supposed to be upholding law and justice in the case of Bob White. But after placing that phony-baloney classified ad in the newspaper, I've got this almost 100 percent-for-sure creepy feeling that Perry's ghost is sending messages through the gorillas to ME, Lily Annabel Watson (LAW).

There's only one thing to do: I've got to go back to the zoo sometime when nobody's around and figure this thing out. But how? How can I break into the gorilla cage at the zoo? And how can I get back to the hotel without anyone noticing? And how can I—

Oh my gosh. Never mind. I have an idea.

THE MENAGERIE HOTEL
Guest Comment Card

October 27

Hi, Robin!

Believe it or not I have another favor to ask you. Actually, this time I have two. But before I ask, I want you to know that if you EVER need anything from me, please ask. I owe you a jillion favors.

Anyway, here goes:

Favor 1: Remember when you told me you were sewing a Halloween costume for someone? Well, do you think you could make a costume for me? I want to dress up as Larry, the little gorilla, on Halloween night—just for fun with the other jurors.

Here's the problem: I'm completely broke. I don't know how much a gorilla suit costs, but I get $10 a week in allowance and I PROMISE I will pay you back after the trial. You can even charge interest if you want. I'm also supposed to be getting $5 a day for jury duty, but I haven't gotten squat yet. I've got plenty of Tyle Tender left and I'd be happy to pay you in that. Which do you prefer—real money or Tyle Tender?

Favor 2: Would you mind taking out another ad for me in the newspaper? The words I want to put in the ad are in the envelope on my desk.

Thanks a 1,000,000 for everything!

Lily

P.S. I don't know what gorilla size I am, but I weigh about 85 pounds.

I.O.U.

You can fill this part in with however much I owe you

⟶ _____ dollars for the

I, Lily A. Watson, owe ROBIN _____
purchase of a gorilla suit and a classified ad in The Tyleville Quill.
I promise with all my heart to pay Robin back in full as soon as jury
duty ends and I start getting my allowance again.
   AND, I promise to buy Robin a shrimp cocktail after the trial. (It's not
a drink. It's cold shrimp you dip in a spicy red sauce. Sounds gross but
it's completely delicious.)

Lily Watson   October 27

Here's the ad I want to
put in The Tyleville Quill.

145

10/27

Lily,

I'd be happy to make a gorilla suit for you. And don't worry about the cost. I can use the material left over from the last costume I made. It shouldn't take me more than a few hours.

I'll try to have the costume to you by tomorrow.

Robin

P.S. Almost forgot: Your advertisement will appear in tomorrow's paper.

The Tyleville Quill

Tyle Publishing
Rhett Tyle, Publisher

50 cents....…....................Saturday, October 28.....…............Morning Edition

Rhett Tyle testifies in tears

Rhett Tyle captivates courtroom

In his compelling testimony yesterday morning at the Tyle County Courthouse, zoo owner Rhett Tyle testified that he sometimes blames himself for the death of Perry Keet.

"I never should have let that sweet boy work with someone as loathsome as Bob White," Tyle told the jury.

Prosecutor Golden Ray Treevor made it clear that Tyle was not legally at fault for Perry Keet's death.

"Just because you grieve the tragic loss of young Perry," Treevor said, "you don't need to feel you're legally responsible for the boy's death."

Tyle, who has not been charged in connection with the murder of Keet, replied, "You're darn tootin' I don't! I'm just a good old country boy who loves animals and children."

Rhett Tyle then burst into tears. Judge E. Gall ordered a one-hour recess for Tyle to compose himself, but the afternoon session continued in the same mournful tone.

Tyle testified that he hired Bob White eight years ago to clean cages and perform various maintenance jobs around the zoo. Tyle said he felt it was his civic duty to employ Bob White.

"I wanted to give the poor guy a chance," Tyle told the jury. "He came to me looking for a job, telling me how much he loved animals. What was I supposed to do–turn the weirdo away?"

According to Tyle, after White allegedly murdered Keet on zoo property, Tyle fired all his security guards and began patrolling the zoo himself, night after night, searching for the boy's missing body.

"It's my life's mission to find that poor boy's body," said Tyle, as he wiped a tear from his eye with a red satin handkerchief emblazoned with a panoramic view of Tyle-O-Tropolis.

Looking back, Tyle said he wished he had never hired "a murderer like Bob White."

After sustaining Mally Mute's objection to the comment that White was a "murderer," Judge Gall ordered the jury to disregard Tyle's remark.

(Continued on page 2, column 2)

Saturday, November 4

Priscilla Parade

AND **ART AUCTION**

What's the Buzz
by
Bernie "Buzz" Ard

So we finally heard from him: Rhett Tyle.

The prosecution's chief witness and local bazillionaire claims his employee killed the young boy. So why don't I believe him?

I don't know. Maybe I should. But how can you trust a guy who made his millions putting live snakes in cakes? Sure, it was a craze. And only one in 100 cakes actually had a rat snake in it.

Still, any man who could think of something as twisted as Snake-in-a-Cake gives me the heebie-jeebies. Lucky for us his next venture failed. Remember his chain of restaurants–Snake 'n Steak?

Please. Not while I'm eating.

But Tyle's an abominable showman, if ever there was one. And don't worry. He's not reading this. Never does, do you, Tyle? See what I mean? He'd rather line the cages at his zoo every morning with my column than read it.

Way back when, not long after Tyle blew into town, I begged *The Quill* editors to let me do an investigative piece on the guy. Snoop into his past. Nose around the old neighborhood in Oklahoma. Gather string. Dig dirt. You know, the usual drill for us muckrakers.

Of course the idea went over like a lead balloon. Probably because Tyle himself green-lights all stories about His Royal Rhettness. And if there ain't a camera (and a purty reporter), furggidit.

So it goes. And like I always say, I've got the perfect face for birdcage liner.

But whaddya make of this? Molar Boy, our resident orthodontist, is now sporting tusks. Yup. One on either side of his mouth. He says he was inspired by the elephants at the zoo. Came back that night and made himself a set of tusks out of wood putty. Says his next project is a set of wombat teeth.

I'm telling you, fiction writers can't make up stuff this good.

"Buzz"

CLASSIFIEDS

Catering for events, large and small. Call Tom. tel: 555-2533

Carry signs. Make money. Good cause. Call Mrs. Goe. 555-KIDS

Homemade pizza delivered to your door. Call Donna and Adam at 555-2889

Hansel: Can we talk on Halloween night? Where? Gretel.

Sewing & alterations. Costumes my specialty. Call

(From page 1)

Prosecutor Golden Ray Treevor continued his line of questioning, asking Tyle to recount the events of last summer. Tyle said he began noticing a change in White in June, when Perry Keet began volunteering as a cage cleaner.

"It's almost like Bob White was jealous of Perry Keet," Tyle said. "It was almost as if he thought Perry was stealing his job."

Tyle testified that Perry came to him on more than one occasion to say that Bob White frightened him. Treevor asked Tyle how he responded.

After a prolonged sob, Tyle finally replied, "I told Perry that this old zoo was all Bob White had in the whole world, and that we had no reason to be afraid of him. But I didn't have any idea what would happen. I didn't know that Bob White would wig out. I didn't know he'd kill poor little Perry. I'm just thankful we have the upcoming Priscilla Parade and Art Auction to look forward to and take our minds off this tragic nightmare."

The defense is expected to begin cross-examining Tyle on Monday.

OCTOBUR 28

I DON NO HOW MISTUR TYLE CAN SIT IN THET CHARE AND LIE LIKE HE DOSE. HE NOS I NEVER KILLET THAT BOY OR ABDUPTID HIM. IF ENNYWON NOS WARE PERRYS BODY IS, I BET ITS MISTUR TYLE.

MISS ANNA PROBABLE NOS TO. MISS ANNA SKARS ME EVUN MOOR THEN MISTUR TYLE. SHEES SNEEKEY. MISTUR TYLE ALLWAYZ TOLLD ME MISS ANNAS WAZ HIS GURLFREEND. BUT MISS ANNA TOLD ME WONS SHE JEST PRETAYNDID TO LIKE HIM FUR THE SNAYKS. THETS NOT VURY NIZ.

I RECKUN THEY PROBABLE FED POOR PERRY TO THE SNAYKS. BUT IF I TOLD THAT, MISTUR TYLE WOOD KILL ME FOR SHORE. AND PROBBLY FEED ME TO THE SNAYKS. THETS JEST HOW HE THINKS. HE NOS I NO WHAT GOS ON IN THET ZOO OF HIS. IT DON SEEM FARE TO ME THAT PEEPUL SHOOD BE ABEL TO GIT AWAY WITH THE THINS HE DOSE. BUT THETS JEST HOW IT IS I GESS.

THESE RATS SHURE ARE GETING FREINDLY. THEY LET ME PET THEM LIKE THEY WUZ DOGS. I WISH PEEPUL TRUSTID ME AS MUTCH AS ANIMULS DO.

MY AUTOBIOGRAPHY
BY
FAWN PAPILLON
CHAPTER ONE

Saturday, after lunch

Oh my. Now this is interesting. Last night while enjoying a little skinny-dipping, I decided to take things one step further. Actually, Madame gave me the idea. I hated to leave her alone in the room again, so I carried her down to the pool with me, reminding her to keep still and quiet.

It was a lost cause. Madame began yipping and yapping at the caged birds surrounding the pool. Fearing that someone would hear her, I flung open the cages and let the birds out.

Need I say it had a magical effect? Just as I suspected, Madame made not another yip. Rather, she curled up on a chaise longue and watched the birds circle above the pool.

I did the same, though I was floating peacefully on my back in the pool. Glorious! What an absolutely exquisite experience to watch those graceful creatures frolic overhead.

Sadly, after an hour of pure bliss, I had to return the poor dears to their cages. If someone finds out what I've been up to, there's no telling what might happen to me—or to the birds.

But here's the strange thing. When I opened the doors to the cages and said, "Come on now, sweeties, back to bed," the birds flew directly into their cages. It's almost as if they understood me. As if they know I will free them for good.

And I will! When the moment is right. I must talk to Lily about this. I'll need her help.

I must confess it's odd to have found a friend in Lily. I've spent the last 50 years avoiding people since it spared me the inevitable disappointment and betrayal.

But if freedom is the greatest gift, perhaps friendship is the second greatest. Oh, Fanny! Now you're sounding like a sappy screenwriter. Washed-up film star finds soulmate in young ingenue. Even Hollywood wouldn't buy this script. Fine by me. They can't have it. This is my best role yet. My comeback!

Making movies was never this much fun.

THE MENAGERIE HOTEL
Guest Comment Card

October 29

Dear Robin,

Like it?

I **LOVE** it! I'm wearing it right now while I write this note. It's so perfect I can hardly stand it. Thank you, thank you, thank you. You're the greatest!

Friends always,

Lily

P.S. I bet EVERYBODY'S dressing as Priscilla and Larry for Halloween this year. Was that other fake fur costume you made for someone at Tyleville Middle School? I bet it was for Claire Carter. She always has the best costumes.

P.P.S. **THANKS AGAIN!!!**

10/29

Dear Lily,

I'm so glad you like the costume. I think it'll look great on you, even though I don't know what you look like.

I haven't had any orders from students at Tyleville Middle School. The only other gorilla costume I made was for Mr. Tyle. He ordered a small gorilla costume last Monday and had me deliver it to the zoo on Thursday.

Hope jury duty is going well. I've been reading about the case in the paper. But of course we can't discuss that.

Take care and happy gorilla-ing!

Sincerely,

Robin

NAME: Lily A. Watson

GRADE: 6

TEACHER: Mr. Holmes

JOURNAL ENTRY FOR: Sunday, October 29, 9:30 p.m.

Talk about some serious monkey business. Here's what I know so far.

FACT 1: Anna Conda and Rhett Tyle are in love, or at least in cahoots, as I saw with my own eyeballs last Monday night.

FACT 2: Also on Monday: Tyle ordered a small gorilla suit.

FACT 3: On Thursday, a new, kid-sized gorilla arrived at the zoo.

CONCLUSION: ?????

Well, I'm not sure what all this adds up to, but I'm going to check it out on Halloween.

Excellent!

I know I'm supposed to be writing my most personal thoughts about my life and junk in this stupid journal, but Bob White's life is on the line here. Nothing personal, but I think it's more important that I concentrate on him instead of making up stuff to put in this blah blah blah journal.

And I'll tell you the truth, Mr. Holmes. When teachers ask us to pour out our souls in these kinds of projects and tell them all our **deep, dark secrets,** most times we just make up stuff anyway. So at least I'm not doing that.*

More testimony tomorrow from Mr. Tyle. I've got to remember to watch Anna Conda and see how she acts when he's answering questions on the witness stand. I've also got to find out what's up with Fawn. She told me at dinner tonight she needs to talk to me privately. Cripes, I hope she didn't find out about Madame's adventure on the fire escape.

The most important thing I've got to do is watch the paper to see if the gorillas respond to my latest question.

*I'm sorry if you don't like some of the things I'm telling you, but it's the truth, the whole truth, and nothing but the truth, so help me God. That's kind of a legal expression, which I'll explain when I get back to school.

The Tyleville Quill

Tyle Publishing
Rhett Tyle, Publisher

50 cents......................Monday, October 30..............Afternoon Edition

Tyle says Bob White was a "reliable employee" ... until Perry Keet arrived

Jurors recoil with horror during Rhett Tyle's stinging testimony

The trial of Bob White continued today with more testimony from White's former employer, Rhett Tyle.

In her cross-examination, defense attorney Mallory Mute asked Tyle to tell the jury what kind of employee White was during his eight years at Tyle Park Zoo.

"He was a good worker," said Tyle, who directly supervised White. "How was I supposed to know he'd turn out to be a murderer?"

After reminding the witness to answer only the questions asked, defense attorney Mute continued, asking Tyle about Bob White's work habits.

According to Tyle, Bob White was a reliable employee. He arrived at work on time and performed his tasks satisfactorily.

"Until," Rhett Tyle said, "last summer."

Tyle said Bob White's behavior became increasingly erratic after Perry Keet began volunteering at the zoo.

"Bob was jealous, I guess," Tyle said. "He knew Perry was a better worker than him."

Before asking her final question, defense attorney Mallory Mute reminded Rhett Tyle that he was under oath to tell the truth.

Then, in a voice that was almost a whisper, Mallory Mute asked Rhett Tyle if he saw Bob White kill Perry Keet.

"Well, uh, no," Tyle replied. "I didn't see the exact moment of death, if that's what you mean. What I saw was Bob White leading Perry by the arm and saying, 'Look-a-here, kid. I'm going to show you something.' Then about 10 minutes later, I saw Bob White all alone, looking guilty as sin. He must've struck quick as a cottonmouth. When I asked where the kid was, Bob said, 'I liked to kill him.'"

A collective gasp was heard throughout the courtroom, forcing Judge E. Gall to bang his gavel repeatedly to quiet the crowd.

Judge Gall adjourned court for the day when juror 11 began weeping loudly and was unable to regain her composure.

What's the Buzz
by
Bernie "Buzz" Ard

Larry laments confinement:
"I'M ALWAYS IN MY CAGE"

Larry the young gorilla displays new sign

Things I can live without:

Women who can turn on the tears like a faucet.

Jurors who discuss their kidney stones at dinner. ("But it was the size of a goose egg!")

Turquoise pinky rings on grown men.

Adults who think kids shouldn't know the truth.

And how about the paper strap I find wrapped around the toilet seat in my hotel room every night? Sanitized for my protection? How about just cleaning the blasted thing, not gift wrapping it?

Am I speaking just for myself, or does anyone agree?

Oh, OK. In that case, I'll keep my lid shut.

Have I reported the latest developments by our tooth sleuth? Or would that be uncouth?

No matter. Our residentist (that's juror 5) told me last night at dinner that he has created more than a dozen sets of false teeth, all patterned after the choppers of animals.

When I asked the obvious question (*Why?*), juror 5 shrugged his shoulders and said, "Guess I just got a little bored with human teeth, that's all."

Says he's been thinking of all the business opportunities for an orthodontist who could give people ANY kind of teeth they want–fangs, tusks, you name it.

When I asked the second-most obvious question (*Huh?*), the orthodontist simply smiled, revealing a mouthful of yellow horse teeth.

Ain't jury duty somethin'?

"Buzz"

Pacing in his cage this morning, Larry the gorilla carried a new sign with the words: "I'M ALWAYS IN MY CAGE."

While this latest hand-painted sign from Priscilla's nephew might impress language scholars, some psychologists are concerned about its deeper meaning.

"I'm worried about the little guy," said Dr. Sylvester "Sy" Kologee, world-renowned specialist in adolescent psychology.

"Larry is clearly manifesting the early signs of ape depression," Dr. Kologee continued. "It's obvious that he needs more space, more freedom, more distance from his aunt Priscilla."

When asked to respond, zoo owner Rhett Tyle curled his lip and scratched his underarms.

"Wise guys, schmize guys," Tyle said. "These so-called specialists can kiss my armadillo. Larry's happy as can be. And why shouldn't he be? We've got the Priscilla

(Continued on page 158, column 1)

(From page 2)

Parade and Art Auction coming up in just five days. We're going to put Larry and Priscilla in the Tylemobile and let them ride down Tyle Boulevard. And let me tell you, Larry's as excited about that as an anteater at a picnic."

OUTGOING LAUNDRY

DELIVER TO:	TYLE DRY CLEANERS
RETURN TO:	THE MENAGERIE HOTEL
GUEST NAME:	ANNA CONDA, ROOM 401
DATE SENT:	MONDAY, OCTOBER 30
TIME SENT:	6 P.M.
PRIORITY:	*A S A P*

Rhett,

Bravo! You were wonderful on the witness stand! That bit about Bob White snacking on the llama food was brilliant!

You always warn against counting your snake eggs before they're hatched, but this case is wrapped up tighter than a boa.

Sssssssssssssoooo . . . what's next? What happens after the trial? Are you still thinking what I'm thinking—a tour of Europe and the Far East with Priscilla?

If so, I hope we'll have time to re-cover our suitcases before we leave. You know I hate to travel with shabby luggage. We'll also need to patch the Tyle-malloon. Isn't King just about the right size for the job?

Please let me know what you're thinking.

Anna

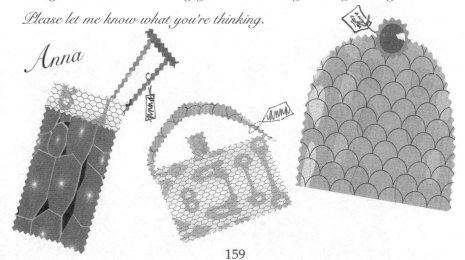

62378

Tyle Dry Cleaners

Sp●ts, Stains and Wrinkles Removed with a Twinkle

Here are your clothes—cleaned to perfection!

PLEASE DELIVER TO:	LAUNDRY RETURNED:
ANNA CONDA ROOM 401, The Menagerie Hotel Tyle-O-Tropolis	⌐6:59 P.M.⌐

Skinny,

Forget *my* performance. Your outburst during my testimony was Academy Award-winning material. You have my vote for Best Supporting Actresssssssssss.

Of course I'm still thinking about our World Tour! Why do you think I paid $1,000 a piece for these passports? We'll leave as soon as the trial is over.

I'm sending a little pocket change to the defense attorney as part of our gorilla warfare. Call it chump change. Ha!

Terrific idea about using King to patch the Tyle-malloon. Let me just fatten him up a bit. Another 100 pounds and he'll be perfect. And what a way to get rid of the chump, too! Going, going, (gulp) gone!

One-hou

<u>New & Improved</u> Strategy:

<u>People who know:</u>

✓   1. Me & Anna ———→ "WORLD TOUR"

(almost) 2. Bob White – going to the slammer

3. The chump
↓
fatten to 100 lbs.
↓
feed to King
↓
skin and patch Tyle-malloon

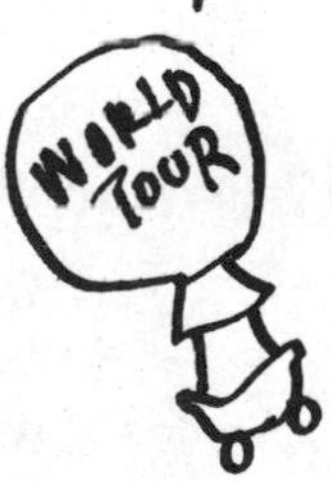

Going, Going, Gone!

WORLD TOUR

MASTER OF THE MARVEL **AMBASSADOR OF THE ENIGMA**

RHETT TYLE

"The Man with the Million-Dollar Smile!" Chief Executive Officer, Tyle Enterprises

From the Penthouse Suite of the Majestic Tyle-O-Tropolis

Tyle Travel	Tyle Isle	Tyle Take-Out	Tyle Turf
Tyle Trends	Tyle & Tyle, LLC	Tyle Tax	Tyle Tackle
Tyle Tile	Hall of Tyle	Tyle Turmeric	Tyle Truffles

October 30

Ms. Mally Mute
Public Defender
Tyle County Courthouse
Tyleville, Missouri

Thought this might come in handy during your next office renovation!

Your pal,

Rhett Tyle

P.S. Don't you have two little boys at Tyleville's Tiny Tots Teachatorium? Gee, I'd hate for anything to happen to them. You still live on Tyle Terrace, right? Last house on the left? I thought so.

NAME: Lily A. Watson

GRADE: 6

TEACHER: Mr. Holmes

JOURNAL ENTRY FOR: Monday, October 30, 11:30 p.m.

I'm *definitely* going to the zoo tomorrow night. The last ad I put in the newspaper asked Hansel (my code name for Perry's ghost) where we could talk on Halloween. Today the little gorilla was carrying a sign that said: "I'M ALWAYS IN MY CAGE." There's **NO WAY** this is all just a big coincidence.

But I've still got to think this thing through. The problem isn't going to be breaking out of here. That'll be easy. I'll just climb out my window and crawl down the fire escape. I'll be wearing my gorilla costume, so I'll look like just another trick-or-treater coming from the big Halloween party in Tyle-O-Tropolis.

But here are my problems:

1. I don't have any real money left for a taxi, so I'm going to have to walk to the zoo, which is on the complete opposite side of Tyle-O-Tropolis. It's more than a mile away. Luckily I found a map of this place, so I'm figuring out the best route.

2. I don't want anyone to see me at the zoo. From what Mr. Tyle said in court on Friday, I know he's the only one in the zoo at night. I've got to make sure he's not there tomorrow night.

The good thing is I have the perfect lure right next door to me. All I have to do is forge an invitation from Anna and mail it to

Rhett. Then, I can write a fake note from Rhett and slip it under Anna's door.

3. So here's the real problem: I know it's illegal to forge someone's name. But what if you do it for a good reason? I think that might be OK, but I'm not sure. I don't want to do something illegal and be sent to jail and have to live in a cell like Bob White. That would be my worst thing—besides writing in this stupid blah blah blah journal which you're not even reading.

Not reading?

✎ THE MENAGERIE HOTEL ✎

Tyleville, Missouri
A Tyle Entertainment Property

10/30

Mr. Rhett Tyle

Tyle Enterprises

Tyleville, Missouri

Dear Rhett,

How about coming over for some trick-or-treating on Halloween night (tomorrow)? Shall we meet at, say, 11 o'clock? You know the place.

Anna

✎ THE MENAGERIE HOTEL ✎

Tyleville, Missouri
A Tyle Entertainment Property

The Menagerie Hotel

Room 401

Dear Anna,

How's my favorite juror? I'm thinking of coming by for some Halloween sweets at 11 o'clock. Same place as last time.

Rhett

The Tyleville Quill

Tyle Publishing
Rhett Tyle, Publisher

50 cents.......................Tuesday, October 31................Morning Edition

Bob White's true confession:
"I liked to kill that boy"

Saving the most dramatic evidence for last, prosecutor Golden Ray Treevor is expected to offer Bob White's confession into evidence tomorrow. In the confession, signed by White just hours after Perry Keet's disappearance, Bob White admits to killing young Perry Keet.

White's confession is critical to the prosecution's case, since there are neither eyewitnesses nor forensic evidence of the alleged murder.

Sources close to the case say the defense will be hard-pressed to overcome this damaging piece of evidence.

Especially troublesome for the defense is the tone of the confession, which contains such phrases as "I liked to kill that boy." The confession will undoubtedly force defense attorney Mally Mute to call Bob White to the witness stand in his own defense.

White's signed confession was obtained by Tyleville police last July and made public during White's preliminary hearing in August.

Bob White and Perry Keet were cage cleaners at Tyle Park Zoo. Keet's body was never found.

That strange Mr. White *(file photo)*

Witness Bob White

A friendless man who lives alone in the woods with more than 30 dogs. A lonely guy who rides an old bike countless miles along the highway each day, burying dead animals.

Suffice it to say Bob White is a defense attorney's worst nightmare.

"The biggest problem with Bob White is his body language," says legal expert Arthur Itty. "He won't look a person in the eye. He looks at his shoes when he's answering questions. His whole body screams, 'I'm guilty!'"

In addition, Bob White signed a confession in which he admitted not only committing the crime but that he "liked to kill that boy."

"Let me put it this way," Itty said. "If I were Bob White, I wouldn't be making any vacation plans at the moment."

What's the Buzz

by

Bernie "Buzz" Ard

Boo!

Did I scare anyone?

Didn't think so. But it's Halloween, for goblin's sake. Think I'll go as a Pulitzer Prize-winning columnist. One thing's for sure. Nobody'd know it was me.

Hey, don't be so quick to agree with the old pen pusher!

I did the math last night and realized I've been churning this column out for 47 years. That's a lotta birdcage liner, folks.

Guess I woke up on the wrong side of the nest today. But then I looked out the hotel window this ayem and saw a squirrel get hit by a Tyle Dry Cleaners delivery truck.

Coulda been you or me, kid.

That's when it hit me like a brick to the forehead. You know, the usual dull thud. But let's get serious for a minute. A young kid dies while this old hack keeps churning out his daily drivel in *The Tyleville Swill*? Where's the justice there?

Oh, don't mind me. I've got a bad case of sequestritis. Too much time alone. Too many hours spent wondering what happened to my life.

And in my free time, I've been trying to figure how this old geezer is fit to judge the fate of another.

Tomorrow's the day we hear from Bob White himself. This is the guy the prosecution will ask us to condemn to death.

Phwew. Talk about trick or treat.

I gotta tell ya, folks. This ain't no party.

"Buzz"

Visitors descend upon Tyle Park Zoo

Attendance at zoo reaches all-time high

Attendance records at Tyle Park Zoo hit an all-time high yesterday as more than 748 tour buses from around the country arrived at the zoo. City officials say the upcoming Priscilla Parade and Art Auction has brought thousands of tourists to Tyleville.

The Priscilla-packed events, scheduled for this weekend, promise to be the biggest celebration this city has ever seen.

ᘓ THE MENAGERIE HOTEL ᘔ
Tyleville, Missouri
A Tyle Entertainment Property

NAME: Lily A. Watson

GRADE: 6

TEACHER: Mr. Holmes

JOURNAL ENTRY FOR: Tuesday, October 31, 6 p.m.

Well, today's the big day. Make that the big night.

I'm halfway scared and halfway excited about all this. If the bailiff finds out I left the hotel, I'll probably get thrown off the jury. If my parents find out, I will definitely be grounded for the rest of the year. And if I've really made a date with a ghost . . . I'm trying not to think about that.

I don't think I'll have any trouble blending into the crowd of trick-or-treaters when I'm in my gorilla suit. But if something terrible happens to me, please tell the police to retrace my steps so they can find my body. If I die, I do NOT want my parents showing stupid school pictures of me at my funeral like Perry's parents did at his. Especially not my third grade picture. I can't even talk about that right now.

Here's my route: ⟶

Remember when I said I was going to have to walk to the zoo? Ha. More like run, paddle, and swing across the Tyle Nile.

WISH ME LUCK!

A MAP

TYLE-O-TROPOLIS

1. THE MENAGERIE HOTEL
   A. WEST WING
   B. EAST WING
   C. TENT ANNEX
2. TOWER ENTRANCES
3. RHETT-UNDA LOBBY
4. BANK OF TYLE
5. LE TYLE
6. SOUVENIRLANDIA
7. BOAT HOUSE
8. CLOCK TOWER
9. WINDMILL RESTAURANT
10. MUSEUM OF ODDITIES
11. LEANING TOWER OF TYLE
12. TV TYLE
13. RADIO TYLE TOWER
14. HOUSE OF S-TYLE
15. NILE-STYLE TYLE

16. AQUARIUM
17. LAUGHATORIUM
18. HIPPODROME
19. TYLE MERCANTYLE
20. FALLING WATERS
21. GROUP SALES
22. EMPLOYEE LUNCHROOM
23. CUSTOMER SERVICE
24. HALL OF TYLE
25. INCINERATOR
26. LOST & FOUND
27. TYLE DRY CLEANERS
28. PERILOUS WHEEL
29. BUMPER CARS
30. THE RATTLER
31. RHETTALINI'S RISTORANTE
32. MOO GOO GI TYLE
33. TYLE PENTHOUSE SUITE

34. AMUSEMENT TENT
35. HAUNTED MANSION
36. WAX MUSEUM
37. CRYSTAL PAL-ICE
38. RHETT'S ROOST
39. CAROUSEL
40. ZOO ENTRANCE
41. JUNGLE BUNGLE
42. CAMEL TENTS

43. PETTING ZOO
44. AVIARY
45. DONKEY RIDES
46. GORILLA VILLAGE
47. REPTILE HOUSE
48. INCUBATORS
49. STABLES
50. WEATHER CREATOR

Information
Elevator
Telephone
Comfort Station
Tyle Tender Teller
Tyle Trinkets
Snax Shax
Restaurant
Pie-Thon Bakery
Tyle Taxi Stand
Tyle Boat Tours
Bridges
Entrance

N

TYLE PRINTING AND PUBLISHING

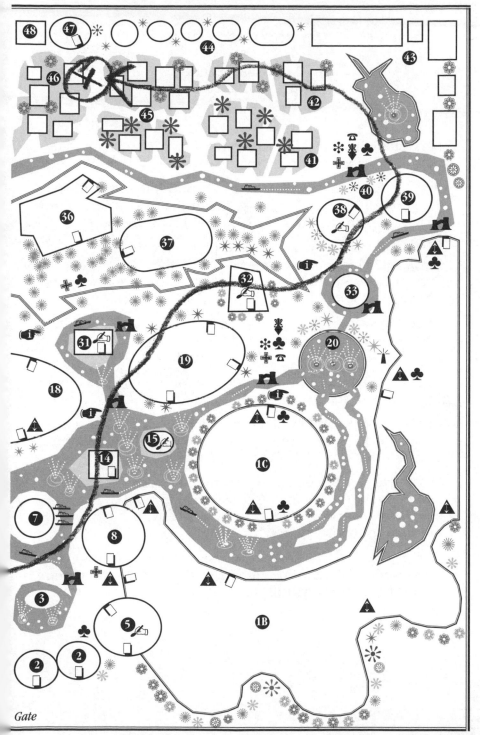

Gate

MY AUTOBIOGRAPHY
BY
FAWN PAPILLON

CHAPTER ONE

Midnight

It's midnight on Halloween and I'm just in from my nightly commune with nature.

And . . . dare I say it? My bathtub is now filled with ducks. Yes, ducks! How could I resist the little fluffs? There were 12 of them stuffed in a cage, one on top of the other.

I let them out of their cages to play with the rest of the birds while I frolicked in the pool. And the precious ducklings followed me into the water! Even Madame was amused, I could tell.

After my swim, I wrapped the little loves up in my towel and fled, naked as a jay bird, up to the fourth floor, where I made a home for them in my bathtub.

I felt terrible returning the other birds to their cages, but I have a plan for their escape.

Can't wait to show Lily my new roommates. I just knocked on her door. No answer. Not even a peep. The dear girl must sleep like a rock. Sign of a clear conscience.

I'll talk to Lily tomorrow about my plan for releasing the rest of the birds in this overgrown cage of a hotel. I'm sure she'll want in on the plot. After all, freeing the birds was her idea in the first place.

But I must take all precautions to ensure that no one–besides Lily and me–knows of the plot I'm hatching OR of the hatched friends circling in my tub.

∽ THE MENAGERIE HOTEL ∽

Tyleville, Missouri
A Tyle Entertainment Property

NAME: Lily A. Watson

GRADE: 6

TEACHER: Mr. Holmes

JOURNAL ENTRY FOR: ~~October 31st~~ Wednesday, November 1, 3:15 a.m.

You're not going to believe this. I just got back from the zoo. Guess who I found there: PERRY! He's alive and perfectly fine. Bob White didn't kill him or hurt him one bit. He's not a murderer. Rhett Tyle is! And he kills animals, not people.

I'm getting ahead of myself. Let me change out of this blasted gorilla suit and take a deep breath and start again.

OK. From the beginning.

I left my hotel room at about 10:30. There was a huge group of trick-or-treaters at a Halloween party down in the Grand Lobby, which was partly good because I blended into the crowd. But it was partly bad, too, because I couldn't see real great under my mask and I kept bumping into people, which slowed me down and freaked me out because I kept thinking I might see someone I knew. (I didn't.)

Anyway, it was almost 11 o'clock by the time I finally got to the zoo. Getting there was the hardest obstacle course of all time. You wouldn't believe how fast you can run when a hippopotamus in the Tyle Nile is looking at you and licking his slobbery chops.

Breaking into the zoo wasn't as bad as I expected. I just climbed over the fence by the Snax Shax. I had to jump about eight feet

174

off the fence, but I had my tennis shoes on under my gorilla suit and landed just fine.

Once I got inside the zoo, I went directly to the gorilla village. That fence was harder to climb, but I made it OK. Then I snuck all the way out to Priscilla and Larry's cage. I stood in front of it for a minute (it seemed like an hour) and whispered: "Hansel? Are you there? It's me, Gretel."

About two seconds later I heard a noise, like somebody laughing under a pillow. Then Larry came up near the front of the cage. He pulled his gorilla mask off his face, and said: "Hey, Gretel. Looks like you need a shave."

Well, it wasn't Larry under the mask. It was Perry! Alive, not a ghost! He let me in the cage and gave me a hug, which was kind of weird, but kind of nice, too. He said he was never so happy to see another person in his whole life. After listening to what he's been through, I believe him.

It's a long story, but Perry is Larry. Perry has to pretend he's Larry. Otherwise Mr. Tyle will kill him. And Bob White didn't murder Perry. What happened was this:

All summer long, Perry had been asking Bob White why the reptile house was always closed. Bob told him to never mind, but Perry kept asking and asking because he's crazy about snakes, just like Mr. Tyle.

Finally, one day when Perry had really been bugging Bob about it, Bob said OK and told Perry to follow him. Perry was really excited. None of us has been in the reptile house since fourth grade because it's always closed for renovations.

Well, when Bob White opened the door to the reptile house, Perry's excitement turned to sick-to-your-stomach **SHOCK**.

Perry says he saw HUNDREDS of snakes (some were 25 feet long), all squiggling around in the bottom of a big pit. And Mr. Tyle was in there, too, standing on a platform above the pit and dropping live rats to the snakes below.

Perry says Mr. Tyle also feeds cats and dogs to the snakes. Why? Mr. Tyle wants the snakes to grow as big as possible—because he skins them!

Where do you think the snakeskins for those dresses and purses and belts at Anna Conda's House of S-Tyle Fashions come from? Yep—the zoo. Couldn't you just die?! I'm getting a . . . million . . . tiny . . . goose . . . bumps . . . just thinking about it.

When Mr. Tyle saw Bob White and Perry watching him, he screamed. Perry couldn't remember the exact words, but it was something like, **"What are you doing in here? I gave strict orders that this building was OFF LIMITS!!"**

The truth was Mr. Tyle was flipping out because he'd been caught red-handed (or rat-handed, I should say) in this snake factory of his.

That's when Mr. Tyle took Perry hostage in the zoo—so Perry couldn't tell anyone what really goes on in the reptile house. I guess Tyle figures Bob White's too stupid to blow the whistle on him. Plus, Mr. Tyle needed someone to blame Perry's disappearance on.

Well, Mr. Tyle put Perry in a secret cage under the gorilla house and fed him goat food. (Perry says it tastes like stale cold cereal with molasses.) The only good thing, Perry said, is that Mr. Tyle let him out of the cage every night on two conditions: 1) Perry had to clean all the cages in the zoo while Mr. Tyle patrolled the grounds, and 2) Perry had to be back in his underground cage by 7 a.m., when the gates to the zoo opened.

After he finished his chores, Perry spent most nights in Priscilla's cage. He's always gotten along real well with Priscilla since she's so gentle. Plus, she knows Perry because he used to clean her cage all the time. He wasn't at all afraid of her. (I wasn't either.)

And guess what Perry did in Priscilla's cage? He painted on the walls! That's right! Those are all Perry's paintings, not Priscilla's. Perry snuck over to the Snax Shax one night and stole a bunch of little mustard, ketchup, and mayonnaise packets. He mixed them together and used them to paint on the cage walls.

Once people saw the paintings and started asking questions about them, Mr. Tyle made up this big giant lie about what a talented artist Priscilla is. That's when Mr. Tyle started throwing blank canvases and tubes of paint in Priscilla's cage and making Perry stay up all night painting.

See what I mean? It's so complicated, it could make your head BURST!

Perry said the paintings are what saved his life. Otherwise, Mr. Tyle would've killed him by now for sure. Tyle's just keeping Perry alive so he'll keep painting the pictures to bring more people to the zoo and make more money for Tyle.

I could hardly believe it. I still can't. I wanted Perry to escape right then and there with me. I told him we could leave the zoo the same way I came and go back to my room at the hotel.

But he wouldn't because of Bob White. Perry said now that one person (me) knows the truth, justice can be done. He said Bob

White is safe because it takes an entire jury of 12 people to convict a person. Perry said now that I know the truth, it's up to me to make sure Bob White is found not guilty.

OK, so this is where it gets a little embarrassing. I started crying. Not big blubbery sobs, but my eyes started burning—like when you open your eyes underwater in a pool with too much chlorine—and my throat felt like I had a fish bone stuck sideways in it.

I said some stupid stuff like, "Why can't YOU just go to the police and tell them the truth? How come I have to do this? This is too hard!"

Perry gave me another hug and said not to worry. It would all be OK. He said this case was way too big and unbelievable for the Tyleville Police. Besides, Perry said some of the police take payoffs from Mr. Tyle, so even if they knew, they wouldn't do anything about it. But if they DID and Mr. Tyle and Ms. Conda found out an investigation was under way, they'd be gone in a heartbeat. *AND* they'd take Perry and Priscilla with them.

I started crying a little bit more when he said that last part. Luckily, Perry didn't hug me again. (Three hugs would've been just plain gross.) But he said now that I'd cracked the case, we could start making plans for exposing Rhett and Anna to the world as the creepy crooks they are. Perry thinks we should do it on Saturday, during the Priscilla Parade and Art Auction, because Mr. Tyle's going to take Priscilla and Larry (really Perry) to the auction.

I've got so much work to do. I don't have time to write or think. I know this is a mess. And no offense, but I have too many other things on my mind to worry about besides a ~~dumb old~~ journal.

178

(Whoops. Sorry about the cross out.)

Perry wants me to come back to the zoo and bring him a radio.
I told him I didn't have one. None of us jurors do. But Perry said
he needs a radio so he can listen to the trial. He told me to
STEAL one from Tyle Trinkets. Jeez!!! Now I'm going to be a
common criminal on top of everything else.

I'll write more later, after I figure out how to get Bob White out
of jail and Perry out of the zoo. Right now it feels like I'm the
one being held hostage. It's like there's a traffic jam going on
inside my brain and everyone's honking horns and yelling out the
window.

I'll think of something if I can just quiet my brain a little. I'm
halfway tempted to tell Fawn all this, but she has a DO NOT
DISTURB sign hanging on her door. I hope nothing's wrong.

Oh, I forgot to tell you one funny thing: Guess how Perry knew it
was me on jury duty? He's been reading Buzz's columns in the
paper. Mr. Tyle always has Perry use newspapers to line the
cages. Anyway, Perry said he could tell I was juror 12 by the way
Buzz described my stupid red hair and the handwalking lessons
I've been giving him. Isn't that wild? Extraordinary!

I've got one more letter to write and then I'm going to bed. I
need to get some sleep because Bob White is going to be on the
witness stand today and I want to be wide awake for that.

THE MENAGERIE HOTEL

Tyleville, Missouri

A Tyle Entertainment Property

November 1

The Honorable Judge E. Gall
Tyle County Courthouse
Tyleville, Missouri

Dear Judge,

Since I didn't get in trouble for the other letter I sent, I guess it's OK to write to you. I hope you and your family are fine. Did you get a lot of trick-or-treaters at your house?

Actually, there's a treat I'd like to ask for. I'm wondering if you'd consider letting the jury attend the Priscilla Art Auction on Saturday. I read in the newspaper that it's going to be the biggest thing EVER in Tyleville.

I'd sure hate to miss it. I think most of the jurors feel the same way. Is there any chance we could all go? Please think about it.

Sincerely,

Lily Watson

Juror 12

P.S. I'm sorry I write only when I want something. It must seem like I'm a brat, which I promise I'm not.

P.P.S. This is more important than you'd even believe.

NUVEMBUR 1

TODAY I HAF TO SIT IN THE CHARER AND ANSUR CWESTYUNS.

MISS MUTE SED NOT TO BE NURVUS SO IM TRYIN NOT TO BE.
BUT IT STILL SCARES ME. SPASHLY HAVIN MISTUR TYLE RITE
THER IN THE ROOM AND MISS ANNA ON THE JURRY.

MISS MUTE SED ALL I HAVE TO DO IS TELL THE TROOTH. THE
ONLY PROBLUM IS I CANT TELL THE HOLE TROOTH BECAWS
THEN MISTUR TYLE WOOD KILL ME FOR SHURE. I TOLD MISS
MUTE THET. SHE SED SHE WAZ SURRY SHE COODENT HELP
MOOR. THEN SHE STARTID CRYING. I SED THETS OK. DON
WURRY. I AXED HER WOOD SHE GO OWT TO MY TRAYLER
AND OPEN SUM MORE BIG BAGZ OF DRY FOD FUR MY DOGZ
AND GIV THEM SUM CAN FOD TO. SHE SED SHE WOOD.

IF THE JUDJ SENDS ME TO THE LECTRIC CHARE, I DON NO WHO
WOOD TAKE CARE OF MY DOGZ OR MY NEW FREINDS THESE
RATS. IM AFRAYD MISTUR TYLE WOOD GET HIS HANDS ON
ALL THE ANIMULS IN THE WURLD AND FEED EM TO HIS SNAYKS.
THAT WOOD BE THE SADDUST PART OF ALL. BEESIDZ PERRY
DYING I MEEN.

GESS I SHOOD EET THIS SANWIDJ FOR BRAYKFUST. BUT IM
TO NURVUS TO EET.

TyleRadio for Tyleville
Transcript
Wednesday, November 1

KEN AIRY: Live from the majestic studios of K-TYLE atop Tyle-O-Tropolis in downtown Tyleville, this is Ken Airy. Let's rejoin the trial of Bob White, where, in a hushed courtroom, the prosecution's cross-examination of Bob White is in progress.

G. R. TREEVOR: Mr. White, you know why you're here, don't you?

B. WHITE: Yes, sir.

G. R. TREEVOR: And why is that?

B. WHITE: Well, I guess there's some people thinks I killed a young boy.

G. R. TREEVOR: Some people think you killed a young boy. Indeed, they do. You're a simple man, aren't you, Mr. White?

B. WHITE: I reckon so.

G. R. TREEVOR: Your attorney has told this jury several times what a simple man you are. A simple man. So let me make this real simple for you, Mr. White. You killed Perry Keet, didn't you?

B. WHITE: No, sir, I --

G. R. TREEVOR: You killed Perry Keet and you confessed to the murder at police headquarters, didn't you?

B. WHITE: I guess I didn't right know what was going on down there.

G. R. TREEVOR: Didn't right know what was

going on? Hmmm . . . Why don't you tell the jury what happened the night you made that confession to the police?

B. WHITE: Well, sir, I'd have to start at the beginning, when they came to get me.

G. R. TREEVOR: Who came to get you?

B. WHITE: The police officers. Mr. Tyle was with them, too. He showed them other fellers where I was.

G. R. TREEVOR: Where were you, Mr. White?

B. WHITE: I was home.

G. R. TREEVOR: What were you doing?

B. WHITE: I was building a couple of new doghouses. I wanted my dogs to have some little houses to live in, with windows to look out of and some rugs on the floor for them to sleep on.

G. R. TREEVOR: And what happened when the police and Mr. Tyle arrived at your home?

B. WHITE: Well, they got out of their car and Mr. Tyle said, "There's the guy who said he liked to kill Perry."

G. R. TREEVOR: What happened next?

B. WHITE: They put some handcuffs on me and put me in the police car. I asked the police officers was I going to be gone a long time. They said maybe. So I asked would they open some big bags of dry food for my dogs. They did. Then we all rode downtown together. Nobody said much of anything until we got to the police station. Then the fellers said they wanted to ask me a couple questions.

G. R. TREEVOR: What kind of questions?

183

B. WHITE: Mostly 'bout Perry.

G. R. TREEVOR: What about Perry?

B. WHITE: They wanted to know if I was friends with Perry.

G. R. TREEVOR: And what did you say?

B. WHITE: I said sure I was friends with Perry. He was a real nice boy. We worked together over at Mr. Tyle's zoo.

G. R. TREEVOR: And you talked with the investigators for a few hours, is that correct?

B. WHITE: Yes, sir.

G. R. TREEVOR: And during that time, you answered their questions honestly and completely?

B. WHITE: Yes, sir, I reckon I did.

G. R. TREEVOR: And did they ask you about the last time you saw Perry Keet?

B. WHITE: Yes.

G. R. TREEVOR: When was that?

B. WHITE: I . . . I reckon it was the day he disappeared.

G. R. TREEVOR: That would be July 24.

B. WHITE: I reckon so.

G. R. TREEVOR: And then you told the police investigators that you "liked to kill" Perry Keet, didn't you?

(SOUND OF GASPS IN THE COURTROOM)

JUDGE E. GALL (sound of banging gavel): Order!

G. R. TREEVOR: I'll repeat the question, Mr. White. When you were asked what you knew about

184

Perry Keet's disappearance, you told police investigators that you "liked to kill that boy," didn't you?

B. WHITE: What I meant --

G. R. TREEVOR: Yes or no, Mr. White. Did you say that the last time you saw Perry Keet on the afternoon of Monday, July 24, you "liked to kill" him?

B. WHITE: Yes, sir.

(SOUND OF COMMOTION IN THE COURTROOM)

JUDGE E. GALL (sound of banging gavel): There will be order in the courtroom.

G. R. TREEVOR: Mr. White, at the end of your conversation with the investigators, you were asked to sign a confession. Is that correct?

B. WHITE: Yes, sir.

G. R. TREEVOR: Is it the confession I'm holding in my hand?

B. WHITE: I reckon so.

G. R. TREEVOR: Did you write this confession yourself, Mr. White?

B. WHITE: No, sir. I said some stuff and they typed it up on a computer.

G. R. TREEVOR: But you read the confession and confirmed its veracity by signing the confession, didn't you, Mr. White?

FROM THE JURY BOX:

JUROR 12: Tell 'em you can't read, Bob! Tell 'em you never made it far enough in school to learn how to read!

JUDGE E. GALL: Order in the courtroom. That

will be enough from the jury box.

JUROR 12: Tell 'em they made you sign something you couldn't read, Bob! And tell 'em what you meant by "liked to kill" Perry. You meant you ALMOST killed him by scaring him to death when you showed him what Mr. Tyle was doing in the rep --

JUROR 11: Oh, good heavens! I think I'm going to faint!

JUDGE E. GALL (sound of banging gavel): Order! Order! Order! Juror 12, one more word out of you and you're off the jury. Bailiff, please attend to juror 11, who seems to have fainted. This court will recess until tomorrow morning, at which time I trust all members of the jury will be composed and silent observers in the courtroom.

(SOUND OF GAVEL BANGING ONCE)

LILY WATSON'S JOURNAL
AND
last minute
RESEARCH PAPER

PART FOUR
What a Mess

I.   Getting in big trouble (with a judge, no less)
II. Getting in big trouble with my parents when they find out I shoplifted a radio
III. Trying to keep my mouth shut during deliberations
IV. The parade and art auction (Going, going, gone!)
V.   Trial by ~~Jury~~ journal

The Tyleville Quill

Tyle Publishing
Rhett Tyle, Publisher

50 cents...................................Wednesday, November 1...................Evening Edition

Outburst in the courtroom!
Juvenile juror reprimanded for disorderly conduct

As Judge E. Gall reprimands juror 12 for disorderly conduct, juror 11 collapses from stress

The first juvenile juror in Missouri history found herself in danger today of being dismissed from the jury hearing the Bob White case.

After speaking directly to White from the jury box, juror 12 was told by Judge E. Gall that one more word would result in her dismissal. If that happens, some legal experts say the judge would be forced by the juvenile juror law to declare a mistrial. Other experts speculate that an alternate adult juror could take the place of juror 12, and the case would proceed uninterrupted.

Critics of the juvenile juror law see today's outburst as proof that the presence of a juvenile on a jury is a dangerous and unnecessary disruption.

"The issues involved in a capital murder case are extremely complicated and deeply disturbing," said Dr. Sylvester "Sy" Kologee, a specialist in adolescent psychology. "Most juveniles are incapable of processing the questions raised in such cases. The stress alone is probably too much for even the most well-balanced child."

"That's what I've been saying all along," said Lynn Goe, president of Protect Our Children from What They Shouldn't Hear or See Organization. "I happen to know this child personally, and I can tell you that she is a fragile flower. I shudder to think what will become of her after this experience."

Goe and her supporters have picketed the courthouse during the Bob White trial in an attempt to force lawmakers to reevaluate the juvenile juror law.

"Isn't it clear that juveniles do more harm than good on a jury?" Goe asked.

The trial of Bob White resumes tomorrow.

"GO LAW"
Larry weighs in on courtroom drama

Just minutes after court recessed today in the Bob White trial, a new painting was discovered in the gorilla cage at Tyle Park Zoo.

"GO LAW" were the words painted in bright colors on a canvas carried by Priscilla's nephew, Larry.

"I'm just so impressed by that little guy," said Iris Ogle, who drove from her home in Walla Walla, Wash. to see the pair of artistic gorillas at Tyle Park Zoo.

"I especially like the way Larry's giving his two cents in that murder trial," Ogle continued. "Somebody should present that little monkey with a key to this city!"

THE HONORABLE JUDGE E. GALL
TYLE COUNTY, MISSOURI

It is the Court's observation that several jurors hearing the Bob White case are experiencing mild to severe stress.

For this reason, I am giving my permission for the jurors to attend the Priscilla Parade and Art Auction on Saturday, November 4. It is my hope that this entertaining and lighthearted activity will calm the nerves of jurors.

Security measures must be in place to ensure that jurors have no contact with family, friends, media, or others who might try to influence their decision in the case of the State of Missouri vs. Bob White.

Judge E. Gall, November 1
Judge E. Gall

NAME: Lily A. Watson

GRADE: 6

TEACHER: Mr. Holmes

JOURNAL ENTRY FOR: Wednesday, November 1, 11:45 p.m.

Boy, I almost blew it in court today. I couldn't help it. The more I know about what's REALLY going on, the angrier I get at Mr. Tyle and Ms. Conda.

I'm also completely ticked off at Perry. I went back to the zoo again tonight at 10 o'clock. I wore my gorilla costume, just like on Halloween, and no one looked twice at me. Perry wasn't even worried about my safety. The only person he ever thinks about is himself. And all he wants to talk about is his stupid funeral. Last night I made the mistake of telling him how many people were at his funeral. Now all he does is ask about every person in our class: Did Matthew come to the funeral? Did Alena? Did Flora? (She's in the #1 popularity group, and I know Perry likes her.)

Cripes. I don't remember for sure who was at the funeral and who wasn't. Of course I didn't tell him the reason I don't remember—that I was too busy thinking about my own funeral and who from our class would be there.

At least Perry was happy that I stole the radio for him, like he asked me to. I haven't stolen anything in forever. (I don't count stealing quarters from my dad's desk at home because he told me I could have those.) But shoplifting a radio from Tyle Trinkets? While wearing a gorilla suit? I will get grounded for LIFE if my parents find out about this.

Fortunately, I had a plan. It dawned on me last night after I got back to the hotel that Perry didn't need any fancy escape plan. All he had to do was wait until there were a bunch of people standing in front of his cage. Then he could just pull his mask off really fast and yell, "HELP, it's me, Perry! I'm not dead! Rhett Tyle is holding me hostage!"

Of course, everyone would be shocked. But they'd call the police or the FBI or someone and throw Mr. Tyle in jail and that would be that.

I told Perry the plan and he just stood there biting his lip. Finally, I said, "It's not that complicated! You can do it tomorrow. What's the big problem?"

That's when he pointed to the ceiling. (Hold on. I've got to crawl under my covers while I write this next part because it's the world's creepiest thing ever.)

At first I didn't understand what Perry was talking about. Probably because I couldn't see it at first. But when I focused where Perry was pointing, I saw it. It looked like a big branch, but it wasn't. Are you ready for this?

Mr. Tyle put a 22-foot **KING COBRA** in a glass cage right above Perry and Priscilla's cage. If Perry makes one false move (like yelling, "HELP!"), Mr. Tyle says he will open the snake's door with a remote control button and the cobra will have the meal of his life.

I took one look at that snake and saw him look back at me and I'm not ashamed to say I jumped straight out of the cage and ran all the way back here without even saying good-bye to Perry.

I am SO SPITTING MAD at Perry for not telling me about that snake. There's no way in the world I would've gone back tonight, which of course, Perry knew. But he wanted his blasted radio. AND he wants me to write a letter to his parents to let them know he's OK. The last thing I heard him say when I was flying out of there was, **"LILY, YOU'VE GOT TO FIGURE OUT A WAY TO GET ME OUT OF HERE!"**

I don't know why I have to do everything. I don't think I've taken a deep breath in a week. Remember when I first got here and was painting in the bathtub? Of course you don't because you're not even reading this blah blah blah journal. If you were, you'd know that I was just like a silly little kid when I started jury duty, which seems like a million years ago.

Now I'm practically a real-life private eye, like in *Harriet the Spy*, which is a good book you should read, if you read books about girls, which most boys don't because they don't want people to think they're sissies, which is completely stupid because anyone who cares what people think of them is a dumb cluck, as Fawn would say.

But *Harriet the Spy* was a book and this is REAL! Here I am risking my neck to crack this case and save Bob White and Perry (the knucklehead) Keet. I shouldn't gripe. Poor Bob White's been sitting in that jail for months. And Perry's been locked up in the zoo, which is even more dangerous than jail.

Before Perry showed me the snake in the ceiling, he told me about all the weird things that have happened to him at the zoo. One night he got chased by a crocodile, which nearly scared him to death. Crocodiles can move really fast, Perry said, but they

192

can't make sudden changes in direction. So if ever you get chased by a crocodile, you have to run in a zigzag.

Perry also got spat on by a camel (he says it had stinky breath) and hugged by an elephant. He said its trunk was really scratchy. He even watched Mr. Tyle hypnotize the zebras one night. Remember I told you how Mr. Tyle hypnotized that duck he took to Buckingham Palace? Well, Perry says Mr. Tyle can hypnotize **ANYTHING**—birds, camels, elephants—by staring into their eyes and saying creepy stuff. Perry's not sure how Mr. Tyle does it, but he (Perry, I mean) says he wants to learn how to hypnotize, too.

But see? This is exactly the kind of cool stuff Perry's learning at the zoo. When he gets out, he's going to be a big fat hero again, just like at his funeral. And I'm going to be grounded. I'll probably end up getting arrested for stealing that radio. And if I have to wear one of those vomitous orange jumpsuits, I will die.

At least if I'm in jail, I won't have to keep this stupid journal. But if I did, I'd make it real dramatic, like that girl Anne Frank who kept a diary during World War II. I love stories about girl heroes, even if they die. I would love to be a young hero like Anne Frank and do something really noble and important. Except if I died, my parents would completely fall apart. At least, they better.

That reminds me of the letter Perry wants me to write to his parents. I guess I probably should. I better write my parents a quick note, too, just to make sure they're still worrying about me enough.

I'll do that later tonight. Right now I've got to go across the hall to Fawn's room. She asked me to come over at midnight. She said she has something really important to tell me. If only she knew the really humongous mess I've gotten myself into. I'll probably have gray hair by the time I'm in eighth grade.

Oh, wait. I just thought of one more reason why I'm mad at Perry. Remember when he told me last night that Mr. Tyle was feeding him goat food? Well, when I went over there tonight, Perry was just finishing a triple-cheeseburger and a strawberry shake. He said he had a whole banana cream pie for lunch.

Mr. Tyle visited Perry this morning on the way to court and told him from now on he can have anything he wants to eat since he's being such a good hostage. Mr. Tyle even brought a scale in to make sure Perry isn't losing any weight. I swear, Perry's getting better treatment than I am on jury duty.

MY AUTOBIOGRAPHY
BY
FAWN PAPILLON

CHAPTER ONE

Very late Wednesday
(or is it very early Thursday?)

Lily just left. I wish I'd had a camera when I opened the door to my bathroom and showed her the ducklings paddling around in my tub!

Of course she asked where the little darlings came from. So I told her. I also told her about my skinny-dipping. Her mouth hung open for a full five seconds. When I told her my idea of freeing the other birds in this hotel, she kissed me. She kissed Madame, too, and then turned a handspring.

I told her I wanted to free the birds quietly tomorrow night, but Lily suggested we open the cages during the Priscilla Art Auction on Saturday.

Imagine, all the birds flying freely out of their cages. I must say, it's an exquisite idea.

And what a statement we'll make! A perfect closing argument. We think alike, Lily and I.

Before she left, she asked to borrow two stamps for letters she's writing. I bet she's a good writer. I may have some work for her before it's all said and done.

A friend

To: **Mr.** and **Mrs. Keet**

2830 Eighth Street

Tyleville, MO

Tyleville NOV 02 MO

34

YOU may not believe this but your son is alive! Unfortunately, he IS in a lot of danger. Don't worry. Someone is looking OUT 4 him & PLANNING HIS escape. If all Goes well, he'LL be HOME after the Art Auction.

a friEND

Mom and Dad,

I'm not supposed to write to you during jury duty, but I wanted to let you know I'm fine. I hope you both are well, too.

I don't want you to worry too much about me while I'm here, but a little bit of worrying would probably be OK.

I've become v. good friends with Fawn Papillon. Maybe we could invite her over for lasagna when jury duty is over.

The food here is pretty good, but not as good as at home.

I miss you both. (A lot.)

Love,

Lily

P.S. There's an orthodontist on the jury who says my teeth are just fine.

LAW

Mr. & Mrs. Watson
221 Baker Street
Tyleville, MO

NOV
02

34

NUVEMBUR 2

THIS IS MY LAST DAY IN CORT.

THE LAWYURS WILL TAWK SOME MOOR AND THEN THE
JURERS GO VOAT. SEEMS LIKE MISS MUTE DOZINT CARE
TO MUTCH ABOWT TRYING TO SAYV MY LIFE ENYMOOR.

MAYBEE SHE THANKS IM GILTY. O WELL. THERES NOT
TO MUTCH I CAN DO ABOWT THET I GESS. I AXED HER
TO PLEASE GO CHEK ON MY DOGZ AND SEE IF THEY
NEED MOOR FOD. SHE SED SHE WOOD.

I WUNDUR IF ILL DIE. I HOPE IT DOZINT HURT TO BAD.
IT STELL SEEMS RONG TO ME THAT SOMEBUDY SO BAD AS
MISTUR TYLE WILL WALK AWAY FREE WHEN PERRY AND
I HAF TO DIE.

LIFE ISNUT FARE I GESS.

Golden Ray Treevor
Prosecuting Attorney

The State of Missouri vs. Bob White

Points to make in closing argument:

Review for jurors:

>*Perry Keet is dead while BW is alive
>*Mr. & Mrs. Keet's pain/loss/sorrow
>*Tyle's testimony–BW had MOTIVE
>*BW's confession–BW retracted only to save his life
>*BW = a simple man BUT a guilty man (and a KOOK!)
>*Your duty and responsibility as jurors is to convict
>*Law, order, the safety of this community is in your hands

YOU MUST CONVICT THE DERELICT!

FROM THE DESK OF MALLORY MUTE
Public Defender
Tyle County, Missouri

Notes for closing argument

* Corpus delicti: the body of a crime—e.g., Perry's murdered body was never found.

* It is agreed by all authorities that when proof of the corpus delicti in homicide cases rests in circumstances (not on direct proof), it must be clear and convincing evidence. Must be proved beyond a reasonable doubt. The State of Missouri has not done this. If you have a REASONABLE doubt about Bob White's guilt, you must vote NOT GUILTY.

* Call the preschool and baby-sitter. Make sure kids stay inside all day.

K-TYLE FM 100
TyleRadio for Tyleville
Transcript
Thursday, November 2

KEN AIRY: Live from the majestic studios of
K-TYLE atop Tyle-O-Tropolis in downtown Tyleville, this is Ken Airy with K-TYLE news on
the hour. Closing arguments were made today in
the Bob White trial. Reporter Maggie Pie is
standing by at the Tyle County Courthouse with
details. Maggie, what was it like in there
today?

MAGGIE PIE: Well, Ken, after listening to the
prosecution's closing argument, there were few
dry eyes in the courtroom. Golden Ray Treevor
asked jurors to picture what Tuesday night
must have been like for Mrs. Eleanor Keet, as
trick-or-treaters came to her door. Halloween
had always been a favorite holiday for Perry
Keet, who loved dressing in costume. Treevor
asked jurors to imagine Mrs. Keet's pain as
she passed out candy, knowing her son will
never again participate in that favorite rite
of autumn. Treevor then asked jurors to think
ahead to an evening two and a half years from
now, when Perry's classmates will graduate
from Tyleville Middle School without him.
He'll never wear a cap and gown. Never go to
college or veterinary school, as he dreamed
of. Never get married or have children. Never
make Mr. and Mrs. Keet grandparents.

KEN AIRY: Heavy stuff, Maggie.

MAGGIE PIE: You can say that again, Ken. It
was an emotionally charged two hours as
Treevor painted scene after painful scene of
what life is like for the Keets now that young

Perry is gone. Judging from the moist eyes of at least six jurors, it was an effective strategy for the prosecution. One juror in particular, juror 11, sobbed almost uncontrollably.

KEN AIRY: And what about the defense's closing statement?

MAGGIE PIE: Well, Ken, as you know, this was defense attorney Mally Mute's last chance to place doubt in the jurors' minds about Bob White's involvement in the disappearance and death of Perry Keet.

KEN AIRY: How'd she do?

MAGGIE PIE: We won't know for sure until the jurors deliver their verdict. But if I had to guess, I'd say it didn't sell. Mally Mute had a tough case to make, especially in light of the signed confession by Bob White. Other than White, Mute didn't call a single witness in his defense. To tell you the truth, Ken, Mally Mute seemed almost resigned to what now appears certain to everyone: that jurors will find Bob White guilty of murder in the first degree and will assess the maximum penalty of death by electrocution.

KEN AIRY: What happens now?

MAGGIE PIE: Finally, after four weeks of not talking about the case, jurors will begin deliberating behind closed doors at eight o'clock tomorrow morning.

KEN AIRY: That's when the real work begins for the jurors, right, Maggie?

MAGGIE PIE: That's right, Ken. Until now, their job has been to be good listeners in the courtroom. Tomorrow they'll move to a private jury room, where they'll discuss the evidence presented in the case and try to arrive at a verdict.

KEN AIRY: Remind us how the voting works.

MAGGIE PIE: To convict Bob White, all twelve jurors must cast guilty votes. If 11 jurors vote guilty and one juror votes not guilty, Bob White is a free man.

KEN AIRY: Sounds pretty intense.

MAGGIE PIE: There's no doubt about that, Ken. Deliberating a capital murder case is an overwhelming experience for anyone. And remember, we have a 12-year-old girl on the jury.

KEN AIRY: How's she holding up?

MAGGIE PIE: Not well. The poor thing has had dark circles under her eyes for the last two weeks. By all appearances, the pressure of serving as a juror has been too much for her. I think it's safe to say the juvenile juror law will be reexamined very closely after this trial. The good news is we're hearing rumors that the judge will allow jurors to take a break from deliberations on Saturday so they can attend the Priscilla Art Auction. It should be a real stress reliever, especially for the young girl on the jury.

KEN AIRY: Thanks, Maggie. I should mention that K-TYLE Radio will carry gavel-to-gavel coverage of the First Annual Priscilla Art Auction. Stay tuned for all the news right here on K-TYLE FM 100.

The Tyleville Quill

Tyle Publishing
Rhett Tyle, Publisher

50 cents...............................Friday, November 3.................Morning Edition

Jurors to begin deliberating today; Reaching a verdict could take hours, days, even weeks

Jurors hearing the Bob White trial will begin deliberations this morning, weighing the evidence against White, which includes a signed confession.

Before they begin discussing the particulars of the case, jurors will select a foreman to preside during the deliberations and to speak for the group when they deliver their verdict to the judge.

It's anyone's guess how long it will take jurors to reach a verdict. Some court watchers predict it could take as long as three days. Others predict an earlier verdict.

"I'm guessing they'll be out in time to enjoy a delicious all-you-can-eat brunch on Sunday at Windmill on Tyleville," Rhett Tyle told reporters.

In the event they do not reach a verdict by noon tomorrow, jurors have been granted special permission from Judge E. Gall to attend the Priscilla Art Auction. The twelve-person panel, plus two alternates, will view the auction from a special roped-off section in the hotel lobby.

Victimized again;
Keets receive cruel letter from local hoaxster

As if losing a son wasn't bad enough, Perry Keet's parents were the victims of a cruel prankster who sent the grieving parents a cryptic note.

Bob and Eleanor Keet received the letter in yesterday afternoon's mail.

"It was mailed locally," Eleanor Keet said. "You could tell by the postmark."

The letter was composed in the style of a ransom note, with words torn from newspaper headlines.

"It said Perry was alive but in a lot of danger," Bob Keet told reporters. "The letter ended by saying Perry would be home after the art auction."

The Keets turned the letter over to the police.

"It was signed 'a friend,'" Eleanor Keet told Police Chief Jay Byrd. "But

Bob and Eleanor Keet give anonymous letter to Tyleville police

what kind of friend would play such a mean trick on us?"

What's the Buzz
by
Bernie "Buzz" Ard

The scene opens as an ensemble cast of jurors enters the deliberation room. The plot thickens. . . .

As I recall from courtroom movies, we'll take an initial vote to gauge the general mood of the jury. The choices? Guilty or not guilty.

But how can I vote to convict a man when there's no convincing evidence? And no, I'm not counting Tyle's twisted testimony or Bob White's forced confession.

Talk about your fangless prosecution.

Oh, and speaking of fangs, guess what kind of choppers juror 5 is sporting these days? You got it: fangs. Says it's the look for the next decade.

But back to the trial: How can I convict a man just because he's an oddball with weird habits. Hey, that could be me! And it's certainly juror 5.

But, folks, since when is being an oddball a crime?

I need to take a stand for the oddball. Juror 12 suggested I take a handstand. During the Priscilla Art Auction.

I gotta tell you, I'm tempted.

But first, the vote.

"Buzz"

Art dealers arrive in Tyleville

Dealers catch a sneak preview of original gorilla artwork, now on display in the Grand Lobby of The Menagerie Hotel

Art dealers from as far away as Sydney and Singapore are arriving in Tyleville to bid on paintings by Priscilla the gorilla and her nephew, Larry.

"I came with two suitcases full of unmarked bills, just like Mr. Tyle told me," said one European art collector, who wished to remain anonymous. "I'll pay whatever it takes to get a masterpiece by Priscilla or Larry."

Art appraisers estimate some paintings may bring as much as $3 million.

NAME: L.A.W.

GRADE: 6

TEACHER: Mr. H.

JOURNAL ENTRY FOR: Friday, Nov. 3, 7:30 a.m.

If you think I've got time to write in this journal, you're nuts. We leave for the courthouse in 15 minutes. At 8 o'clock, we'll finally start talking about the trial. I've got to keep my **big fat mouth** shut and not tell the other jurors what I know about what *really happened* to Perry.

This is going to be the hardest part, but Perry made me swear that I'd wait until the Priscilla Art Auction, which is tomorrow. Otherwise, he says Mr. Tyle will push the button and open the cobra's door, which I had nightmares about last night, thanks to Perry.

It really bugs me the way Perry thinks he's the only one who's in any danger. What about me? What about Bob White? I swear Perry only thinks about himself. I do, too, but I try not to do it out loud, just to myself and in this blah blah blah journal. I haven't had time to do my teeth exercises or practice my handstands or anything in forever. And I STILL haven't had one lousy shrimp cocktail since this trial started.

But never mind all that. I've got a plan to give Mr. Tyle and Ms. Conda a taste of their own snake oil medicine tomorrow at the art auction. Fawn's going to help me. She thinks I'm helping her with her plan to free the birds. But if all goes as planned, we'll be helping each other.

Until then, my main job is to make sure the jury doesn't convict Bob White before tomorrow's auction. We haven't talked about the case one iota, so I have no idea what anybody else thinks. What if I'm the only one who thinks he's not guilty? How am I going to convince the others without telling them that Perry is alive?

And what if it flies out of my big mouth without me realizing it, like the time my mom told me a million gajillion times not to say anything about the goiter on Uncle Mel's neck. What do I do when he walks in the front door of our house, but blurt out, "Cripes, Uncle Mel! What's that big old completely gross purple blob on your neck?"

I am such a loser sometimes, it freaks me out. I have GOT to concentrate today so I don't louse up this whole thing.

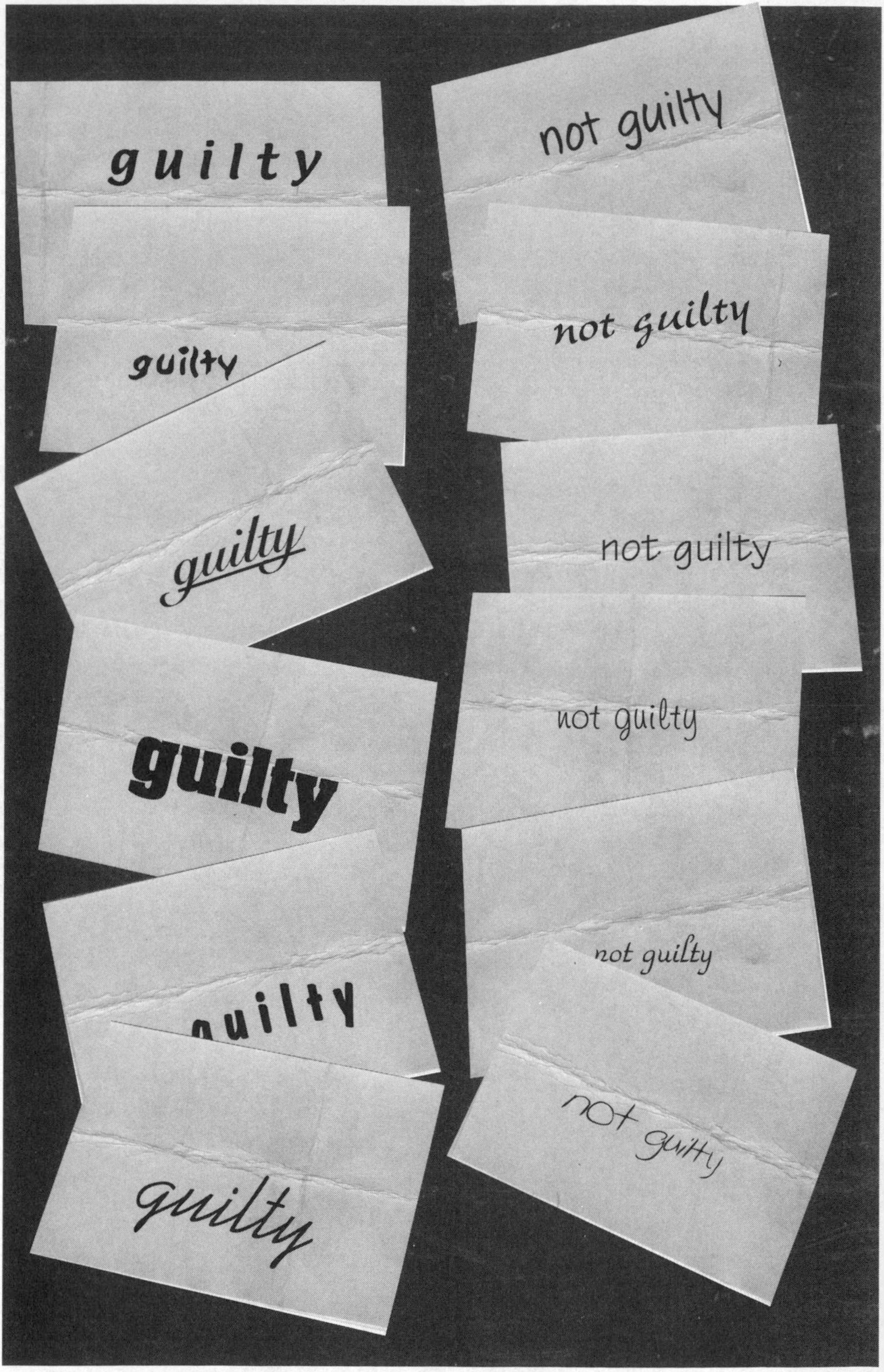
guilty
not guilty
guilty
not guilty
guilty
not guilty
guilty
not guilty
uilty
not guilty
guilty
not guilty

OUTGOING LAUNDRY

DELIVER TO: TYLE DRY CLEANERS
RETURN TO: THE MENAGERIE HOTEL
GUEST NAME: ANNA CONDA, ROOM 401
DATE SENT: FRIDAY, NOVEMBER 3
TIME SENT: 5:20 P.M.
PRIORITY: *URGENT!!!!!! RUSH!!!!!!*

Rhett,

Disaster! We just took our first vote: six guilty, six not guilty. We've got to get out of here. Quick!

Anna

65532

Tyle Dry Cleaners

Sp●ts, Stains and Wrinkles Removed with a Twinkle

Here are your clothes—cleaned to perfection!

PLEASE DELIVER TO:

ANNA CONDA
ROOM 401, The Menagerie Hotel
Tyle-O-Tropolis

LAUNDRY RETURNED:

⌐6:19 P.M.⌐

Pack your bag and bring it with you
tomorrow to the art auction.

It's time for our Great Escape.
Remember the 1988 World Tour? The
Grand Finale. Right in front of their
eyes!

You'll know when the time is right.
GOING, GOING, GONE!

R.A.T.

One-hour service guaranteed with a smile . . . or my name isn't Tyle!

FROM THE DESK OF RHETT TYLE

In the Penthouse Suite of the Majestic Tyle-O-Tropolis

Things to do before tomorrow

✓ Pack clothes, passports,
  promotional posters, etc.

✓ Order helium   (RUSH!)

✓ Tune up Tylemobile

✓ Open sunroof on Tyle-O-
  Tropolis

✓ Test fire Tyle-malloon!

~~Feed the thump to King~~

~~Patch Tyle malloon~~

* No time to patch the malloon.
Will have to take thump with
                                    m.

Egress
here

X park
T-M
here

LOBBY

T-M enter here

The Tyleville Quill

Tyle Publishing
Rhett Tyle, Publisher

50 cents..................................Saturday, November 4..................Morning Edition

SPECIAL PRISCILLA PARADE AND ART AUCTION COLLECTORS' EDITION

Schedule of events

9 A.M. **PRISCILLA PARADE** begins at **Tyle Park Zoo**

Watch the animals from the zoo

PARADE ☆ PRANCE ☆ PROMENADE

through the streets of Tyleville,

followed by the

 MAIN ATTRACTION

Priscilla and Larry, riding in the famous Tylemobile!

NOON **ART AUCTION** begins in the **RHETT-UNDA**

of the Grand Lobby in **The Menagerie Hotel**

Come see Priscilla and Larry and watch as their

EXOTIC ※ QUIXOTIC ※ MACROBIOTIC

ORIGINAL GORILLA WORKS

are sold to the highest bidder

(CASH ONLY, PLEASE)

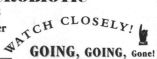

WATCH CLOSELY!

GOING, GOING, Gone!

Bob White trial update; deliberations continue

Jurors in the Bob White trial will continue deliberating today behind closed doors. Sources close to the trial speculate that jurors likely took an initial vote on Friday morning as a starting point in their deliberation process.

Today will be spent discussing the testimony of various witnesses. Jurors will spend their lunch hour in the lobby of The Menagerie Hotel, enjoying the Priscilla Art Auction.

NAME: Lily A. Watson

GRADE: 6

TEACHER: Mr. Holmes

JOURNAL ENTRY FOR: Saturday, November 4, five o'clock in the morning

I might as well forget about getting any sleep. I've been up all night thinking about yesterday and worrying about today.

We started yesterday by voting for one of the jurors to be the spokesperson for all of us. That was easy. Everyone wanted Buzz. Then we took a secret vote on Bob White. It came out 6 guilty to 6 not guilty, which was 2 perfect 4 words! After the vote, Anna Conda started babbling about how she was convinced to the core of her soul that Bob White is a murderer. I felt like saying, "You mean your rotten apple soul!" but I kept my lip zipped.

We have to go back to the courthouse again this morning to continue deliberating. Then at noon, we go to the art auction. Cripes, that's only seven hours away! I'm trying to figure how this is all going to work. If any little thing goes wrong, it could mean curtains for Perry Keet and Bob White. And probably me, too, especially if my parents find out about all this.

My plan keeps changing by the minute. Nobody knows anything about this except me. I'm a nervous wreck keeping it all to myself, but who can I tell? Nobody—because I don't want to risk getting thrown off the jury OR messing up Perry's escape.

I guess the only person I can talk about my plan to is this dumb, stupid journal, which I STILL HATE WRITING in, by the blah blah blah way. I wonder if Anne Frank secretly hated writing in her journal, and if she did the blah blah blah trick to see if anyone was actually reading it.   I think not.

The only reason I'm still even keeping this dang journal is that in case I die before I get out of here, I want everyone to know what REALLY happened.

Whoops. There's Fawn at my door. Time for our morning constitutional. Then breakfast. Then . . . My heart is beating a hundred miles an hour. I've got that feeling you get at the pool when you climb the ladder all the way to the top of the high dive and then decide you want to turn around and climb back down.

Except I can't. This is do or die.

K-TYLE FM 100
TyleRadio for Tyleville
Transcript
Saturday, November 4

KEN AIRY: Live from the majestic studios of
K-TYLE atop Tyle-O-Tropolis in downtown Tyleville, this is Ken Airy with K-TYLE news on
the hour. Well, folks, it's a picture-perfect
day for the First Annual Priscilla Parade
and Art Auction. Looks like Mr. Tyle even
cracked the sunroof on Tyle-O-Tropolis, letting a little fresh air into the complex.
K-TYLE TV reporter Maggie Pie has been covering the Priscilla Parade all morning from
the lobby of The Menagerie Hotel. Maggie,
what can you tell us?

MAGGIE PIE: Ken, close to 20,000 people
turned out this morning for the First Annual
Priscilla Parade, which ended over an hour
ago. The sight of every animal from the Tyle
Park Zoo riding in colorful circus wagons
down Tyle Boulevard was something to see.
And of course the highlight of the parade was
when Priscilla and her nephew, Larry, rode by
in the fabled Tylemobile. It's something I'll
remember for the rest of my life.

KEN AIRY: Where are Priscilla and Larry now,
Maggie?

MAGGIE PIE: Tyleville's beloved gorillas are
in a golden cage, just off to the side of
Rhett Tyle and not far from the jurors in
the Bob White trial, who were given a break
from their deliberation proceedings so they

215

could attend the art auction, hosted by Rhett Tyle.

KEN AIRY: Mr. Tyle is wearing a lot of hats today, isn't he, Maggie?

MAGGIE PIE: That's right, Ken. Tyleville's first citizen and zoo owner served as the grand marshal in this morning's parade. For the last hour, he's been auctioning off the gorilla artwork.

KEN AIRY: We've been hearing rumors for weeks that high-flying art collectors were prepared to pay big bucks for Priscilla's and Larry's paintings. Just how much are they spending, Maggie?

MAGGIE PIE: Plenty. A Priscilla original titled *Come Visit The Zoo* just sold for $1.3 million in cash. And the funny thing is when the painting sold, Larry did a little jig, almost as if he was delighted by the high price.

KEN AIRY: Amazing, Maggie. Though there's not much about those gorillas that isn't amazing. I think we all stopped being surprised by those artful little fellas --

MAGGIE PIE: Ken, if I could interrupt for a minute. Rhett Tyle just placed the final painting to be auctioned on the block. During the last commercial break, Tyle told me that the bidding on this final painting, entitled *LAW Remember Me*, would be very exciting.

KEN AIRY: Maggie, tell us briefly how the bidding works.

MAGGIE PIE: Rhett Tyle will give a brief description of the painting and then start the bidding at $500,000. The painting goes to the person who offers the highest cash bid. I'll zoom in with my Tyle-Cam so the folks at home can listen.

RHETT TYLE (to the crowd): And now, ladies and gentlemen, we come to our final painting of the afternoon, *LAW Remember Me*. Look closely, if you will, at the fine details of this painting. Note the dark, foreboding quality. The texture. The colors. The mood of the moment. Now, ladies and gentlemen, children of all ages, I direct your eyes right here, please. Right at my eyes. Move if you must so that your eyes are looking directly into mine. That's good. Isn't that nice? It's been a long morning, hasn't it? And you're starting to feel a little sleepy, now, aren't you? It's all right. Close your eyes for just a moment. That's all it takes. Just close your eyes.

KEN AIRY: Maggie, what's going on down there?

MAGGIE PIE: Ken, this is going to sound a little strange, but it seems we're taking a short break from the bidding to . . . well . . . I'm not exactly sure what's going on, but three people standing near me are all snoring.

KEN AIRY: Snoring?

MAGGIE PIE: I know it sounds odd, but . . . (yawn) . . . Oh, forgive me. (yawn) You can't imagine how sleepy I've suddenly become. If it's okay with you, Ken, I'm just going to (yawn). . . I'm just going to stretch out here for a minute and take a little catnap.

KEN AIRY: Maggie, this is a live broadcast!

MAGGIE PIE: Don't worry, I'll keep my Tyle-Cam turned on. Good night.

RHETT TYLE (to the crowd): That's right. Get comfortable. Curl up like a little kitty cat if you like. You are all sooooooo tired. It's been such a loooooooong day. You're getting very sleepy. Very, very sleepy. And when I snap my fingers, you'll be sound asleep. Are you ready?

UNIDENTIFIED GIRL FROM THE JURY SECTION: Don't listen to him! He's trying to hypno-tize us, just like he did with that duck he took to Buckingham Palace. It's a long story and I'll tell you all about it later, but don't listen to him! I mean it! Fawn, Buzz, Leon, Dr. L. E. Font. Please, don't even look at him!

RHETT TYLE: Quiet over there! Ladies and gentlemen, pay no attention to the pipsqueak in the corner. Now, when I snap my fingers, you will fall asleep. You will sleep sound-ly, peacefully, with no memory of what has taken place here today. You will not wake up until a loud noise awakens you. Are we ready?

UNIDENTIFIED GIRL FROM THE JURY SECTION: Don't listen to him!

RHETT TYLE: I said QUIET! Anna, grab the loudmouth kid and let's go. The rest of you are listening very closely to what I say.

You are

     Going,

       Going,

         GONE!

(SOUND OF FINGER SNAPPING)

UNIDENTIFIED GIRL FROM THE JURY SECTION:
Ayyyyyyyyyyyyyyyy! Help me! Fawn! Buzz!
Leon! Somebody, please!

(SOUND OF LOUD CRASH)

TRANSMISSION TOWER FAILURE

*   *   * S I L E N C E *   *   *

The Tyleville Quill

Tyle Publishing
Rhett Tyle, Publisher

$1.50.................................Sunday, November 5...................Morning Edition

Perry Keet, Tyleville's youngest hero, is reunited with parents

PERRY KEET IS ALIVE!
Tyleville boy remarkably well after three-month hostage ordeal

To Mr. and Mrs. Keet, the news was both terrible and wonderful.

"To think poor Perry's been locked up in a cage all this time," said his father, Bob Keet. "It's the sickest thing I've ever heard."

But when the Keets saw their son pull a gorilla mask off his face in the Rhett-unda of The Menagerie Hotel, they cried with joy.

"It was a dream come true to learn our son isn't dead," Eleanor Keet said. "Still, taking a child hostage and keeping him in the zoo is simply beyond belief. What kind of person would do such a thing?"

Rhett Tyle and Anna Conda, to name two people.

The two Tyleville residents have been charged with kidnapping, fraud, and cruelty to animals and children. They will remain behind bars at the Tyle County Jail pending their trials.

Judge E. Gall is meeting with attorneys in the Bob White case this morning to discuss a procedure for immediately releasing White from jail and dismissing the jurors from sequestration.

Federal authorities arrived in Tyleville late last night to begin investigating Tyle, Conda, and their worldwide trail of crime and corruption. Documents related to the case are expected to be subpoenaed later today and submitted to a county grand jury.

Rhett Tyle and Anna Conda "framed" at art auction;
"Great Escape" foiled by jurors and birds

Rhett Tyle and Anna Conda's attempted escape through the top of Tyle-O-Tropolis in their hot air Tyle-malloon was grounded, thanks to the work of Tyle's fine-feathered enemies.

A juror in the Bob White trial, identified as screen legend Fawn Papillon, released the countless birds Tyle kept in cages in The Menagerie Hotel lobby. Once free, the birds flew directly toward the motorized balloon

and pecked at it aggressively until it deflated. The Tyle-malloon landed with a crash in the middle of Tyle-O-Tropolis, toppling the K-TYLE radio tower and assorted statuary in the Grand Rhett-unda.

Also toppled, but not broken, was the juvenile juror, identified as Lily Watson. Watson was taken aboard the Tyle-malloon briefly and suffered a sprained ankle during

(Continued on page 2, column 1)

What's the Buzz

by

Bernie "Buzz" Ard

Was your phone jumping off the hook last night? Mine too. Too bad I'm still stuck here on jury duty and couldn't answer it.

But, folks, was that some show yesterday? And to think I had a front-row seat on the whole thing.

No, no, no. Please. Hold your applause. It was no great accomplishment. All you had to do was stand on your hands.

See, Tyle was able to hypnotize most of the crowd with his eyes, using a trick he stole from an old snakeskin flick. But being upside down, I avoided eye contact with the old snake charmer. Thanks to our juvenile juror for that suggestion!

Speaking of Lily Watson, is she a kick in the pants or what? This pint-sized sleuth solved the case right under our own eyes. She even put Rhett Tyle, the diabolical inventor of Snake-in-a-Cake, behind bars. Now there's something I'd pay money to see.

Oh yeah, money. Remember that? Green paper stuff? Comes in handy now and then? Those of us who made our living as serfs in Tyle's empire may soon be looking for new employment.

Well, woop doop di do. What should the old blabbermeister do? Haven't got a clue. But I know one thing: It's high time this old dog tried a new trick.

Woof!

"Buzz"

(From page 1)

the crash landing. Doctors at the scene wrapped the ankle for Watson, who returned to sequestration after a lengthy interview with federal investigators.

Perry Keet was unharmed in the crash. The 11-year-old boy is being hailed as Tyleville's youngest hero for surviving his three-month hostage ordeal.

Shocking pictures reveal Tyle and Conda's true monkey business

Keet and Watson explain Tyle and Conda's monkey business to federal authorities

From phony paintings to snaky sofas, Rhett Tyle and Anna Conda had a regular snakeopoly on Tyle County.

At the request of federal authorities, Perry Keet and Lily Watson led investigators on a guided tour of Tyle's and Conda's businesses. The tour began at a massive snake pit in the reptile house at Tyle Park Zoo and ended at a showroom filled with exotic leather goods at House of S-Tyle Fashions. Along the way, Keet and Watson explained the wretched process Tyle used to raise snakes at the zoo and then skin them for Conda's line of leather products.

"We've never seen anything like it," said FBI agent Alfred Peacock. "This makes Jack the Ripper look like an Eagle Scout."

While searching for evidence at Tyle-O-Tropolis late last night, federal investigators discovered a feeding schedule for Tyle's snakes, whose diet included rats trapped by Tyle Exterminators. Perry Keet was on the feeding schedule for next week, as were dogs owned by former defendant Bob White.

Also at Tyle-O-Tropolis, federal investigators uncovered yet another twist to Tyle's tale of corruption.

"You could say we found a snake in the grass," said Agent Alfred Peacock. "Only it wasn't in the grass. It was in the food. Tyle used snake meat at his restaurants in Tyle-O-Tropolis."

(Continued on page 224, column 1)

Art auction fetches $5.2 million; Money given to artist Perry Keet

Art dealer says he'll never sell painting

The $5.2 million collected by Rhett Tyle during Saturday's art auction was confiscated by Tyleville police and given to Perry Keet, the young artist who painted the now world-famous canvases while he was held captive at Tyle Park Zoo.

"Five million dollars?" asked the incredulous Keet, when he learned the news. "That's amazing, especially considering I got only a B minus last year in art."

When asked what he would do with the money, Perry Keet said he planned to buy his parents a new restaurant.

"And I'm going to have a big party," said Keet. "The whole town of Tyleville is invited. I want to show everyone my ideas for a new zoo."

The art dealers and collectors who bought the young boy's paintings, thinking they were created by gorillas, were given the option of returning the paintings for a full refund.

"Are you crazy?" asked one international art collector who wished to remain anonymous. "Why would I return this painting? It's even more valuable now."

(From page 2)

The news came as a shock to Tyleville residents, many of whom dined at Tyle's eateries.

"Leave it to Tyle to hide behind fancy language," said Dr. Dick Shunary, professor of linguistics at Tyle University.

"What do you think the 'ophidian' was in Emperor Rhett's Ophidian Delight?" asked Shunary. "Ophidian means of or pertaining to snakes."

Snake-in-a-Cage: Tyle's latest invention

Rhett Tyle's final invention was, without a doubt, his most sinister. Some might even call it "cagey."

Tyle used a device he called Snake-in-a-Cage to hide a 22-foot king cobra in the glass ceiling above the cage Perry Keet shared with Priscilla the gorilla. To prevent Keet from escaping during the hostage ordeal, Tyle wired the young boy with sensors and motion detectors. One false move by Keet, and Tyle was prepared to use a special remote control unit to open the glass ceiling and release the snake.

"If he tries to take flight, he'll be a cobra's delight!" was the advertising jingle Tyle told investigators he was working on to market Snake-in-a-Cage as a security device for "businesses, schools, and even home use."

Tyle used a smaller device called the Porta-Python to discourage Keet from escaping during the Priscilla Parade. On a recent trip to Washington, D.C., Tyle applied for patent protection for both Snake-in-a-Cage and Porta-Python.

Designer Anna Conda admitted to police that she was developing a smaller model suitable for evening use. She intended to market it as Boa-in-a-Boa.

Investigators have also learned that Tyle's tale of landing by accident in Missouri nine years ago during a tornado is a lie. Tyle arrived with his longtime partner in crime, Anna Conda, who was hidden in a secret compartment in the Tyle-mallon. The pair, who used a string of aliases to conceal their true identities, chose Missouri as their new home only after they were denied landing rights by 49 states and the District of Columbia.

Missouri has no law banning residency for convicted snake bakers. A bill is expected to be introduced in the next legislative session.

SUBPOENA--DUCES TECUM

In the Circuit Court of TYLE COUNTY   CRIMINAL DIVISION

TO _____LILY A. WATSON_____ AT ____9 O'CLOCK AM__
YOU ARE HEREBY COMMANDED, That setting aside all manner of excuse and delay, you be and appear in proper person before the Judge on the ___10th___ day of _____November_____, then and there to testify and the truth to speak, in a certain matter in controversy now pending in our said Court, wherein __THE PEOPLE OF THE____ STATE OF MISSOURI__ is Plaintiff and __RHETT TYLE and ANNA__ CONDA__ are Defendants, on behalf of the Plaintiff; and you are further commanded to bring with you and then and there produce in evidence*

_____Your jury duty journal_____

----
and hereof fail not at your peril.

WITNESS my hand as confirmation of our said Court that this was done at office in _____Tyleville_____, in the county aforesaid on this ___5th__ day of _____November__.
By _____
Circuit Clerk TYLE COUNTY

*Describe the books and papers to be produced

RETURN

I hereby certify that I have just served the within Subpoena in the County of Tyle and State of Missouri, on the 5th day of November by *hand delivering it to the kid at her hotel room at The Menagerie Hotel. Problem is, she says she needs the journal for some school project. Can't the judge cut her a little slack? After all, this kid DID crack the case.*

_Lane Henn____ , Sheriff
Tyle County, Missouri

225

NAME: Lily A. Watson

GRADE: 6

TEACHER: Mr. Holmes

JOURNAL ENTRY FOR: Sunday, November 5, 11 a.m.

Well, Mr. Holmes, this is it. My last journal entry. I'm going to have to make it quick because I've got to pack my suitcase. Checkout time at the hotel is noon. But what are they going to do if we're late? Throw us in jail? With Mr. Tyle and Anna Conda?

That's right. Those two snakes are behind bars this morning at the Tyle County Jail, thanks to Fawn, who let the birds out of their cages. My original plan was to have the birds peck Rhett's and Anna's eyeballs out so I could trap them in the birdcages. But the birds attacked the Tyle-malloon instead, which turned out just fine, even though I ended up with a *sprained* ankle.

The good news is that Bob White is a free man. He and Perry rode their bikes over to the hotel this morning and had pancakes with all the jurors.

Bob White was back in his old grimy clothes. He still has his *old man smell*. He probably had it all along, but he was sitting so far away in the courtroom I couldn't smell it. The biggest change in Bob White is that he's riding a brand-new bike, which Perry just bought him this morning.

Perry, as you probably know, is a millionaire. He told me he's going to buy Tyle Park Zoo and turn it into a wildlife refuge. He's also using some of the money to buy his parents a new restaurant. He wants to call it Café Mongoose because the mongoose is one of the few animals that are good snake catchers.

We found out from the police that Mr. Tyle was trying to fatten Perry up so he could feed him to that **22-FOOT KING COBRA** in the glass ceiling. Then, Mr. Tyle was going to kill the cobra and use its skin to patch the Tyle-malloon. Perry nearly threw up when he heard about that.

In a way, I think it serves Perry right for not telling me about that stupid snake the first night I was there. In another way, I think it's **completely creepy** how this whole thing turned out being like our *Hansel and Gretel* play in second grade–only the horror movie version of it. I tried to explain it to Perry, but he didn't get it. Then again, he wasn't trying to get it. All he can think about is getting his $5.2 million.

I told Perry he has to return the radio I stole for him. I also told him he absolutely has to put shrimp cocktail on the menu at Café Mongoose. He said he would. He also said I could eat for free at his restaurant with my friends and family and anyone I wanted (like Robin) for the rest of my life.

Perry and I talked about how weird it will be going back to school. He said it's going to be worse for him because now he knows who went to his funeral and who didn't.

I think it'll be ten times worse for me since I have to turn my journal over to the court because of a stupid subpoena–which, if you're reading this, Judge E. Gall, I think is completely UNFAIR. (And speaking of unfair: Perry, if you're reading this, forget the free food. How about throwing some of that $5.2 million this way since I'm the one who saved your sorry rear end?)

What this subpoena means is that everything I wrote about pushing my teeth back and Perry's hugs (which, let the record reflect, I did NOT enjoy one little bit) and my problems with the air conditioner and Uncle Mel's goiter . . . it's ALL going to be made public and used as evidence in the trial against Rhett Tyle and Anna Conda.

Am I going just a little bit crazy at the thought of everyone reading my journal? Yes. Fawn tells me I shouldn't give a flying fig who reads my journal. It was nice of her to say. And I'm sure if it was her, she wouldn't care. That's just how she is.

I, however, am not that cool. And that's never going to change. Well, maybe in eighth grade it will get better, but certainly not in sixth grade. I DO care what people think about me, thank you very much.

So here's what I don't get: I want to be popular and I'm not. Fawn doesn't care about being popular and she is. Perry doesn't do anything but be in the wrong place at the wrong time, and he gets $5.2 million. How fair is that, Judge E. Gall?

Oh well. This is not one of those stories where everyone learns all these big fat important life lessons and goes on to live happily ever after. I've still got crooked teeth and stupid red hair, which Fawn calls strawberry blonde but everybody at school calls orange, which drives me nuts.

So the moral is, even when big things happen, the little things—which SEEM big—never really change. For example, Kim Illion (juror 6) just knocked on my door and asked if I wanted her to French braid my hair for the portrait Leon's going to paint of us before we leave.

And last night, Sandy Piper (the row-row-row-your-boat teacher juror) gave me a little (b)roach she made. It says "World's Lil-est Juror." Can you hear me screaming in my mind? But that's what I mean about the little things never changing.

Oh, I almost forgot one good change: Fawn's giving me an after-school job. I'm going to help her write her autobiography! I can't wait to see her house, especially the aviary. That's a house for birds. Fawn's taking all the birds from the hotel home with her. (As she says, who's going to stop her?) And she's hiring Bob White to build an aviary for them—without cages, of course. He's going to help her feed the birds, too, every day.

Well, I better sign off now so I can finish packing. I need this journal back by November 10th to take to court, so please just grade it and get it over with it.

Unless I hear otherwise I'll assume you didn't actually read this blah blah blah journal. But even if you did, I don't want you to think I learned anything by keeping this journal, because I didn't.

Lily Watson

The End

P.S. Ugh!! I just remembered today is Sunday. I don't really have to come back to school tomorrow, do I? All I want to do is go home and sleep in my own bed for a whole week and maybe do a 10,000-piece puzzle with my mom and dad. I just hope you're not one of those teachers who sends work home when kids miss school.

If I'd only known . . . .

THE TYLEVILLE QUILL
An Employee-Owned & Edited Newspaper

50 cents   **Monday, November 6**   **Morning Edition**

Keet family hosts reunion party for jurors and friends at new Café Mongoose

The reunited Keet family hosts grand opening of Café Mongoose

Perry Keet unveils plans for his Wildlife Refuge & Animal Paradise

"I think the animals will be much happier in their new homes," said Keet, who spent three months in captivity working on an animal-friendly design for the new zoo.

Juvenile juror heralded by legal experts

At a symposium entitled "Our Dear Watson: How Juveniles Are Our Last Best Hope for Reforming the Judicial System," legal experts from across the country heralded Missouri's juvenile juror law and its poster child, Lily Watson.

Lily Watson writes the book on juvenile jury duty

"Lily Watson has become the textbook example of just how valuable a juvenile on a jury really is," Supreme Court Justice Thurgood Marshmallow told conference participants. "By keeping her jury duty journal, Miss Watson has essentially written the book on the importance of including juveniles in the judicial process."

The symposium ended with participants forming the How to Leverage the Wisdom of Juveniles to Bring Common Sense Solutions to Adult Nonsense Organization, or HTLT-WOJTBCSSTANO for short.

Bernie *"Buzz"* Ard to leave *The Quill*

Bernie "Buzz" Ard, Tyleville's man-about-town and *The Quill's* long-time columnist, announced at last night's party that he is leaving *The Quill*.

"I've got a novel to write," Buzz told the crowd at Café Mongoose. "And I'm not getting any younger. I figure I've hidden behind my column long enough. Time to take off the shackles of a daily deadline and give this Great American Novel thing a whirl. Now or never!"

Buzz Ard hinted that the people and circumstances surrounding the Bob White trial might figure in his novel. When asked if he had a tentative title for the book, Buzz replied: "How does this sound: *Snakes, Cakes, and Walking Toothaches?*"

Buzz to pursue career as novelist

Rhett Tyle and Anna Conda behind bars at Tyle Park Zoo

Tyle and Conda are the newest attractions at Tyle Park Zoo

In an unusual twist to Tyleville's most infamous crime saga, Judge E. Gall ordered Rhett Tyle and Anna Conda moved from cells at the Tyle County Jail to cages at Tyle Park Zoo.

"I might lose my robe for this," Judge Gall told reporters. "But it only seemed right to put Mr. Tyle and Ms. Conda behind the same bars they used to detain poor Perry Keet."

Tyle and Conda will remain at the zoo until their trials.

CLASSIFIEDS

Im goin to rite won moor tiem in this diaree just to say evreething turnd owt OK. Bettur then I evur cooduv imajuned.

I thawt no won wood buleeve thad I dinnut kill Perry. I thawt mistur tyle wood git away with evreething. But it dinnut tern owt thet way.

Miss Mute vizided me in jell beefour I left. She sed she waz sorey. She sed she thawt mistur tyle waz the reel killur. She waz afraid he waz going too kill her childrun. thets why she stopt trIng to sayve my live. I sed Thets OK. I unnerstand. Peepul haf to wach owt for there childrun. And miss mute wacht owt fur my Dogz when I waz in jell and coodent. I rolld her we were evun and evreething was OK now.

Im Jfst hapy Lily waz on thet jury. Shes the won who figgered owt wat waz goeng on. She riskd hur life for me. Its all becaws of Lily that perrys aliyve and Im Free.

I asd Lily how in the wulrld cood I evur thaynk her. I asd hur did she want me to bild her a play-haws or sumthing. I told hur—I.O.U. my life.

233

NO WAT SHE SED SHE WANTID? SHE WANTS TO TEETCH ME TO REED AND RITE BETTUR. SHE SEZ THET WOOD BE THE BEST THING I COOD DO FOR HUR. SHE SEZ THAR AR ALL KINDZ OF BOOCKS AND MAGUZYNS ABAWT DOGZ I COOD REED.

MAYBEE SHEZ RITE. BUT ALL I WANT TOO DO RITE NOW IS GO HOME AND SEE MY DOGZ AND FICKS THEM THE BEST MEEL OF THERE LYVES.

IN AWAY ITS FUNY. I ALLWAYZ THAWT PEEPUL DINNUT TRUST ME GOOD. BUT IT TERNS OWT THEY DO. I ALLWAYZ THAWT MY DOGS WERE MY ONLEY FRENDS. SEEMS LIKE I WAZ RONG.

I THINCK ILL GIVE THIS DIAREE TO LILY AS A PRAYSENT.

Bob White

TYLEVILLE MIDDLE SCHOOL
REPORT CARD

November 9

STUDENT NAME: Lily A. Watson
TEACHER: Mr. S. Holmes
GRADE: 6
QUARTER: First

ENGLISH: incomplete
MATH: incomplete
SOCIAL STUDIES: incomplete
SCIENCE: incomplete
FRENCH: incomplete
P.E.: incomplete
ART: incomplete
MUSIC: incomplete

SPECIAL SIXTH GRADE REQUIREMENT:
RESEARCH PAPER: A+

COMMENTS: For reasons beyond her control, Lily did not complete her regular classwork this quarter. However, given her extraordinary efforts in the pursuit of truth and justice, she will receive an A in all subjects.

(And about summer school: Never mind!)

Teacher signature: MR. S. Holmes

P.S. I thoroughly enjoyed your blah blah blah journal.

"Poetic Justice"
11-30
Leon D. Vinci

MY AUTOBIOGRAPHY BY FANNY PIGEON

As told to Lily A. Watson

CHAPTER ONE

Many people think my success came at an early age when I was a child star. But the truth is, I never experienced true happiness until the ripe old age of eighty-two.

That was the year I made friends with a young girl who lived across the hall from me while we served together on a jury. During the trial I also met Bob White, a man more like me than anyone I'd ever met. Mr. White now lives in the guest house of my estate and cares for my birds.

How I became friends with Bob White is a long story, so I'll start at the beginning. . . .

ACKNOWLEDGMENTS

With special thanks to our esteemed panel of jury consultants,

Bill Corsa
Topper Glass
Ruth Katcher
James Klise
Kate Millington
Matthew Willis

and to our mother, Marjorie Klise, who taught us how to pull a research paper together (with yarn!) in one night.